THE PULL OF THE MOON

Elizabeth Berg is the author of the *New York Times* bestsellers *Never Change* and *Open House*, which was an Oprah's Book Club selection in 2000. *Joy School* was selected as American Library Association Best Book of the Year, and *Talk Before Sleep*, another *New York Times* bestseller, was shortlisted for the ABBY award in 1996. The winner of the 1997 New England Bookseller's Award for her body of work, she is also the author of *Range of Motion, Talk Before Sleep, What We Keep* and *Until the Real Thing Comes Along* which were all bestsellers in the United States. A former nurse, she lives in Chicago.

"*The Pull of the Moon* should be read by anyone who has ever
threatened to run away from home. It is wise and witty,
thoughtful and exhilarating. It leaves the reader observing life
with great hope and satisfaction."
Jill McCorkle, author of *Creatures of Habit*

D0494741

The Pull of the Moon

Elizabeth Berg

arrow books

In midlife, we're left with all that was ever ours to hold in the first place.
                                        Barbara Lazear Ascher,
                                            The Habit of Loving

Upon being asked if she knew how to be fifty, Joni Mitchell answered, "It will make itself known."

ACKNOWLEDGEMENTS

My editor, Kate Medina, read this book in installments and kept calling to say she loved it. This was rocket fuel to the fingers. Lisa Bankoff has a cool head, a warm heart, and a great sense of humor – an unbeatable combination in an agent. Jean-Isabel McNutt copy-edits with artful precision and with enormous sensitivity. Thanks too to Sally Hoffman, Renana Meyers, Linda Pennell and Abby Rose for the excellent work they do for me.

My Tuesday morning writing group was with me every step of the way, as usual. My thanks to Sally Brady, Betsy Cox, Linda Cutting, Alan Emmet, Alex Johnson, Kate Kruschwitz, Mary Mitchell, Rick Reynolds, and Donna Stein for their honest input. And for their love.

Last, but most: Thanks to my daughters, Julie and Jennifer, for being themselves; and thanks to my husband, Howard, who tolerates all my travels – inside and out.

THE PULL OF THE MOON

Dear Martin,

I know you think I keep that green rock by my bed because I like its color. And I do like its color. But the reason I keep it by my bed is that oftentimes I wake up frightened, and it comforts me to hold it then. I squeeze it. I lie on my side away from you and I squeeze the rock and look out the window and think that outside are rocks just like this one, lying still and strong and silent. They are beside rivers in Egypt and in fields in Germany and at the center of the desert and on the moon. The rock seems to act as a conduit, drawing out of me whatever it is that is making my heart race, whatever is making me feel as though my own soul is one step ahead of me, saying don't come. Don't bother. Martin, I am fifty years old. The time of losses is upon me. Maybe that's it. I don't know. I saw Kotex in the drugstore the other day and began to weep. Then I saw a mother with a very little girl, helping her pick out crayons, and this, too, undid me. I had to leave without buying what I came for. I drove home and I thought about Ruthie standing next to me as I lay on the couch one day. She was two and a half, holding Legos in the basket of her hands. I had a mild case of flu; I was mostly just exhausted. And Ruthie dropped the Legos on me and used my chest to build a small city and I was perfectly happy. I think I even knew it. It was that Chinese thing, that when your mind is in your heart, you are happy.

You know, Martin, when Ruthie was a freshman in high school, I was driving home from the grocery store one day and listening to the radio and I all of a sudden realized that in four years she would be gone. And I felt like screaming. Not because I have nothing else in my life. Just because she would be gone. I pulled over and I wept so hard the car was shaking, and then I repaired my makeup in the rearview mirror, and then I came home and made dinner and I never said a thing about it, although maybe I should have. Maybe I should have started telling you then. I was afraid, I think, that you would say, "Well, she'll *visit*," and the feeling would have been of all my eggs being walked on by boots.

I'm sorry the note I left you was so abrupt. I just wanted you to know I was safe. But I shouldn't have said I'd be back in a day or two. I won't be back for a while. I'm on a trip. I needed all of a sudden to go, without saying where, because I don't know where. I know this is not like me. I know that. But please believe me, I am safe and I am not crazy, I felt as though if I didn't do this I wouldn't be safe and I would be crazy.

I have no idea what will happen next. I am in a small

Holiday Inn one hundred and eighty miles from home. I have a view of the pool. Beside me I have a turquoise journal, tooled leather, held close by a thin black strap wrapped around a silver button. I bought it the day before I left. Normally, that kind of thing would not appeal to me. But it seemed I had to have it. I opened it, looked at the unlined pages, closed it back up and bought it. It was far too expensive, forty dollars, but it seemed to me to be capable of giving me something I'd pay more for. I thought, I'm going to buy this journal and then I'm going to run away. And that's what I did.

I don't mean this to be against you. I don't mean any of it to be against you. Or even about you. I have felt for so long like I am drowning. And we are so fixed in our ways I couldn't begin to tell you all that has happened inside me. It was like this: I would be standing over you pouring your coffee and looking down at your thinning hair and I would be loving you, Martin, but I would feel as though I were on a ship pulling away from the shore. As though the fact of your sitting there in your usual spot with cornflakes and orange juice was the most fantastic science fiction. I would put the coffeepot back on the warmer and sit opposite you and talk about what was in the newspaper, and inside me would be a howling so fierce I couldn't believe the sounds weren't coming out of my eyes, out of my ears, from beneath my fingernails. I couldn't believe we weren't both astonished – made breathless – at this sudden excess in me, this unmanageable mess. There would a couple of times I tried to start telling you about it. But I couldn't do it. There were no words. As even now, there are not. Not really.

I'll call Ruthie. I'll tell her. You can tell everyone else anything you want. I mean this kindly, Martin.

I'll write you often. I don't want to talk. Please. Well. You know, I write that word *please* and I don't have any idea what to say after it. But please. And can you believe this? I love you.

Nan

I think the last time I had a diary I was eleven years old. At the top of every page, I would say what we had for dinner. That was the most interesting part. I thought filthy was thilthy. "Todd Lundgren is thilthy!" I wrote. Because I saw him at a party putting his hands up Maria Gonzales's skirt. She was wearing nylons and her garters were sticking out because her skirt was pushed up so high.

Well, this is probably not what I should say.

But why not.

I know a woman who tapes pictures in her diary, presses flowers in it, she has the clipping from when John Lennon was shot. Well, she says, it's mine, for me, for whatever I want.

I bought this black pen for you. I feel shy saying this, as though we are friends too new to exchange anything without it being too important.

I have a picture to give you, too. Here is a forties photograph of a woman that I found in last Sunday's paper. She is seated on the grass, wearing a suit and a hat, her purse centered in her lap. She is smiling, but her eyes ache, and behind her, I know this, her hands are clenched. She can't relax. She has forgotten the grass. I kept staring at her, thinking, this is me. Checking my purse three times for keys before I leave the house. Stacking mail in order of the size of the envelopes. Answering the phone every single time it rings, writing "paper towels" on the grocery list the second after I use the last one. I too have forgotten the grass. But I used to do one-handed cartwheels and then collapse into it for the fine sight of the blades close up. And there was no sense of any kind of time. And I was not holding in my stomach or thinking what does my opinion mean to others. I was not regretting any part of myself. There was only sun-rich color, and smell, and the slight give of the soft earth beneath me. My mind was in my heart, anchored like a bright kite in a safe place.

I think I will not use a map. And I think I would like to stop at a house now and then and ask any woman I find there, how are you doing? No, but really. How are you doing?

Dear Martin,

Well, here it is. The first morning. I had such a scary dream last night. Some men had broken into the house and they had tied another man down on to the dining-room table – no one I knew – and they wanted me to help them torture him. It was worse than being tortured myself. The man on the table reached toward me with his fingers, that's all he could move. And I stood stock-still, unable to do anything, and I was filled with a terrible fear because I knew that if I didn't cooperate I'd be killed. I woke up, but I didn't open my eyes, I lay there breathing fast and shallow – I thought I was home, having another bad time.

I thought, I'll say very quietly, "Martin, I had a bad dream," and I was hoping you would take me in your arms and the feel of your undisturbed flesh would be enough to ground me, you wouldn't have to speak. But then I thought, no, it doesn't make sense to wake him, it's only a dream, he wouldn't want me to wake him. And then I remembered where I was and I opened my eyes and turned on the light and saw this ordinary square of motel room, this bland and functional place where sleep is business. I thought oh my God, what am I doing here. And I felt so ashamed, Martin, and I got dressed and packed my suitcase and put my purse over my shoulder – I cried, remembering you had given it to me last Christmas, and had asked me in a way that was nearly shy was that the right one – and I was going to come home, but then I thought, well, it's four in the morning. I'll wait. And I went back to sleep in my clothes, my car keys in my hand, and then when I woke up I didn't want to come home anymore. I wanted to get some breakfast and go on. It has always been true of me that the mornings are my strong time. I wonder if you know that.

I will write to you again tomorrow.

Love,
Nan

P.S. If I'm not back in a week, you should water all the plants. Please don't ignore them out of anger towards me. You needn't do the little cactus on the kitchen windowsill. That one can wait a long time. I have so often wondered how it does it. The leaves are not so thick, you know. On rare occasions, it even blooms. You might want to pay attention, so that if it happens, you don't miss it.

I am preoccupied with my body. Overly watchful of change. It's like being a teenager again, without the cuteness. Without the promise. Without the immense naïveté. Imagine, I used to stare at photos in magazines that highlighted throats and thighs and think, what? What about it? It's just a neck. It's just a leg. Last night I stood in the bathroom on the edge of the tub so that I could see my whole self in the mirror over the sink. I can't remember the last time I had the courage to do that. I remember Elizabeth Taylor saying she once stood naked in front of a full-length mirror – kind of by accident – and that's how she realized how fat she was and she went on one of her famous diets. No chocolates. Only diamonds. When I looked in the mirror in that awful fluorescent light, I saw the age in my body all at once. I saw that the tops of my legs are sagging, like knee-socks falling down, that my belly is lower than it was, and my breasts. Of course, my breasts. I held them up in my hands, making a hand bra, pushing them high up, but they didn't look sexy because the skin on my throat, on my chest, is beginning to get crepey and does not want breasts in its way. It wants flannel nightgowns against it. It wants a woman who is on an archaeological dig and has no time for caring about how it looks. I saw that there is more gray in my pubic hair. The first time I saw a gray pubic hair, I was horrified. I plucked it out, which hurt. And then there were three and four and five and six. And one day I got the laundry marker and colored them in. I'd thought it was time for sex, that we'd probably have sex that night, and I hated the thought of Martin against gray pubic hair. After I did that, colored my hairs like that, I thought, this is not the way to do it. Dyed hair. Moisturizers and exfoliants and wrinkle removers and toners all lined up in my bathroom drawer. My thinking has been misdirected. Somewhere, something is holding the sides of its head and screaming. Still, I went out that afternoon and bought more. Things made with hormones and placentas and who knows what all. The woman behind the counter said "Well, my dear, the effects of aging are not entirely inevitable. It's just a matter of taking care of yourself. It can be done. Look at Sophia Loren, doesn't she look great? You can bet she uses everything. Why shouldn't you? I always say, 'You don't have to be a star to look like one.'"

I bought everything that insane woman told me to buy. I spent two hundred and thirteen dollars and forty-seven cents, I remember. And then I went to the bookstore, to the poetry section, to find something about the beauty of older women and I found nothing. I drove home, and when I got in, I threw the bag of stuff away. With the receipt. Shameful. That is shameful. I should confess it. I should kneel

*down right now and say I am sorry. I regret this awful
waste of things and I regret this awful way of thinking.*

*There, I just did it. I got on my knees and I said that. I
closed my eyes like I was praying but I let my hands hang
loose and open at my sides. Because it is only me talking to
myself. And it felt good. Though the carpet is awfully dirty,
I must say they don't knock themselves out cleaning here.
There were rings on the night table, and I had a vision of
some businessman sitting at the edge of the bed in his
underwear, smoking, drinking his beer, flicking the TV
through all it offered. There was a sex channel here. Martin
watches those channels when he goes on business trips, but
he won't pay. He watches for a minute until it starts
blinking and then he switches channels. From blow jobs to
the home shopping club. Some similarities, actually. I
asked him, Don't you get nervous, waiting for it to start
charging you? I imagined the checkout clerk's lips pressed
tightly together the next morning. But he said no, he pretty
much knew by now when the blinking would start. I said,
"But you . . . so fast?" "After," he said. "You do it after."*

*My friend Janet once told me how when she was on a
trip she watched one of those movies for a while,
masturbated to it. But what turned her on was the women.
She is not interested in women sexually, but she said the
men's penises were all throbbing and purple and veiny and
who wants to watch them come? Apparently they do. But
anyway, the next morning all it showed on her bill was
"movie" and she was so relieved. Imagine a motel at night,*

its walls suddenly removed. How many guests would be watching movies whose dialogue is "Oh baby, that's good, that's good, oh yes." Is there a director on these films? Does he slam his clipboard against his thigh and say, "Cut! Cut!" Did he go to film school? If you stood behind him at the grocery store, would you suspect anything?

Martin and I have tried these movies. It works, which is a sad thing. Of course, we never watch the whole movie. We laugh at the music, make many nervous snide remarks about the dialogue, then get a little quieter, watch a bit more and then we're at it. I wonder what he's thinking. I wonder if he's making me the woman in the movie. For myself, I am thinking, well if she can do that, I can do this! I don't know when sex changed for us. For me, anyway. It used to be a natural completion to a natural attraction. Now I am so ashamed of my body, I don't want any lights on, I don't want to call attention to anything. I need a jump-start to have sex, the excuse of a movie or a martini. Sometimes, even when I'm loosened up, I'll suddenly think of how we look, two middle-aged people, going at it. I'll feel like I'm floating above us looking at our thickening middles and thinning hair and flabby asses and any desire I had will feel like it's draining out the soles of my feet. I'll think, what are we doing? Why are we doing this? Martin will be moving against me, moaning a little, and I'll be thinking, I need to clean that oven.

When we're through, we'll go down to the kitchen for a snack, and I'll think, this is how we are most affectionate, when we stand hip to hip spreading mustard on bread, feeding each other bites of Swiss cheese and smoked ham. Why not skip the other part?

Well, it's time to go to wherever I'm going. But I have to do something first – a favor. This morning, I went for breakfast in the motel dining room and the waiter began rather suddenly talking about angels. I had mentioned the moon because it had still been out, that wispy kind of disappearing moon, a blue-white collar – and he said, oh are you a moon person? I had no idea what that meant, really, and yet I answered, yes I was. And he said he was too, and that also he was an angel person. I said is that right, and I was waiting for him to ask what I wanted, which was French toast, but he didn't. He kept talking about how angels were such a strong feminine presence in his life and that the moon was feminine too, of course. I began looking around a bit to see if anyone else thought he was a little crazy, but then I thought, well, I'm not in a hurry. It's not a bad thing to talk about angels.

I remembered when Martin and I went to Paris and we were in a very small restaurant, maybe four tables, and the waiter there began to tell us about his wife learning to ride a bicycle at age thirty-eight – he spoke wonderful English – but Martin made the tiniest movement with his wrist and the waiter saw, and knew, and stopped talking about his wife and told us about the specials. I was sad about that, I'd been interested in him, a French person telling a French story. I'd thought, I'll bet if I were here alone, he'd have told

me a lot about his family, about himself. As it was, I felt
that Martin was in charge, that the city belonged to him
and he was letting me hold on to one edge of it like I held
on to his hand. Like the young children I saw out on a field
trip one day holding on to a rope.

But anyway, my waiter told me how he saw angels in
dreams and they never spoke but it seemed to him they
were getting ready to, and then he all of a sudden
remembered what he was supposed to be doing and he
asked me what would I like. And I said, French toast, which
seemed so mundane, considering, and he said, oh that was
a good choice, that was his favorite. And I said, well why
didn't he join me, apparently I was the only one in his
station. He got this look, and he played around nervously
with his collar and then he said well he'd love to. And he
came out with two platters of thick-cut French toast —
extra-large servings, he said, winking — and he sat down
with me and tucked his napkin into the neck of his shirt and
then — why not? — I did the same and we began eating with
some relish. And then the manager came over and said,
"Lawrence, what do you think you're doing?" And there
was this awful stillness, the couple across the room holding
their forks midair. I started to say something and the
manager — so young, actually impressed with himself —
said, no no, I'm asking Lawrence. And Lawrence said, why,
he was eating breakfast. And after a moment the manager
said he was fired. Right now. I said, wait a minute, I asked
him to join me, he didn't have any other customers. I was

getting kind of excited like when a good fight starts. Lawrence said no, it was his fault, he's always had trouble with boundaries. He asked would I mind giving him a ride home, though, he didn't have a car, he'd never had one because he didn't understand how they worked. I said, well you don't have to understand how they work to drive one. He said, how can you just assume such amazing things, get behind the wheel trusting your life to this car not knowing anything about it. I said, well, you fly don't you? and he said yes but that he understood perfectly well how airplanes worked. And anyway, he wasn't driving the plane. (The manager was still standing there, and you know he suddenly seemed like the silly one, just standing there with his winter-white arms crossed, his cheap watch ticking on his wrist, while Lawrence and I talked about . . . well, I don't know, the philosophy of technology or something.)

Anyway, the point is, I think this is sort of wondrous, this event. I do. And there is no one to check it out with, no one to pass or fail me for my observation and this is a vast relief. I feel such a lifting inside. Hope, I think. I'll bet Lawrence has angels everywhere in his house, moons hanging from his ceiling. I intend to see. Suddenly time is time. I'm leaving a twenty-dollar tip for the maid. I have always wanted to do that. It makes sense to me. And anyway, Martin and I have too much money. We have for some time. At first it was just that we didn't have to worry about whether we could go out to dinner at some fancy place. Then we got way ahead on tuition, on the mortgage, on everything. We made bigger donations to more organizations. Then he started investing. I never wanted to know about it. I found it sort of frightening.

We buy things over and over again. New cars, before the new-car smell has gone from the old one. New furniture, new silverware, the latest fashions that are sometimes out of style before we've taken the price tags off, more, more, always more, full boxes coming in, empty boxes going out, for what? So that we can sit out on our (new) deck in the summer and drink vodka and tonics out of our vodka-and-tonic glasses with limes that have been cut with the (new) lime cutter? It's always bothered me, what we lost when we stopped being able to fit our things into the trunk of our car. Martin doesn't believe me. He says it's a luxury of being rich to wish you were poor. I don't want to be poor. I just want to be appreciative.

Twenty-five years ago, when I met Martin, he was a hippie. He had a ponytail, tied neatly in the back with a piece of rawhide that smelled like incense. We did drugs once in a while, we used to hurry to clean the kitchen before we came on to the acid, we didn't like coming down to dirty dishes. In those days, Martin talked about angels too. About parallel universes. About the industry of ants, the wisdom in the dance of the honeybee. I would sit on his lap, my long hair streaming down my back, my long dress on and my long earrings, too. I was braless and barefoot, and

Martin and I were filled with wonder at the way the dust motes were colored, we'd never noticed.

I do have to go now. It's almost checkout time. I wonder where I'll eat lunch.

Dear Martin

I hope you've gotten a little bit used to this, to my being away. I have, suddenly.

I am here in a room in someone's house, in a very small town called Midgeville. When I asked at the gas station this evening where the nearest motel was, the man said there was no motel in town, but that the Lewis family had a kind of bed-and-breakfast, real nice place. You didn't get your own bathroom or anything, but you got a bedroom. Twelve dollars. So I came here and it's the most wonderful place. An older couple I'd put in their mid-seventies lives here, and the house is full of the old-fashioned things I love – doilies, a grandfather clock, maple end tables crowded with photos and flowered porcelain dishes, overstuffed sofas and chairs with soft pillows tossed here and there. The bed I have is a beautiful brass one, a blue-and-white quilt on it. The front window looks out onto the garden – I can't really see much now, but Mrs Lewis told me it's her husband's hobby, his pride and joy, he's got sixty different kinds of rosebushes out there. One variety produces silver blossoms! She said she put them in a vase with the purple roses, that they're lovely together.

I feel a little like a child again, up in my room, the door closed, listening to the sound of voices below me. I'm looking forward to the morning – Mrs Lewis is making applesauce muffins and I know they'll be served with some care. My job is only to receive.

I drove for such a long time today, and I don't really get tired. This surprised me – you know how I always used to fade out after an hour or two when we took turns on a trip. But I went for miles and miles, listened to radio stations come in and out, thought about what it would be like to live in each town I passed through – there, the grocery store with the woman in pink curlers coming out, that's where I'd shop; there, the small stone library, that's where I'd request bestsellers from the gossipy librarian. I love doing this, Martin, I used to try to explain to you, why I wanted to take the side roads. But you were always interested in saving time, so we took the interstates and there was never anything to look at, not even telephone poles. When you take the small roads you see the life that goes on there, and this makes your own life larger.

I stop whenever I want to, for as long as I want. Today I browsed in an antique store and I went into a dress shop to try on a yellow skirt I saw in the window and I stopped at a farm stand and bought a big fat tomato and then sat in the car and ate it from my hand like an apple. Then I just sat there watching people for a good half hour or so, seeing who came and what they bought, watching kids yank at parents' hands or quietly rearrange the peaches. I listened to the sound of paper bags being rolled shut, the cash-register drawer dinging open and then being pushed closed. I liked this. You would never have stood for it. I remember once when we were in New York and we passed a man making pizza in a window, throwing the dough high up in the air. I wanted to watch and you lasted about fifteen seconds and then we had to move on. I could have stood there all night. We are so different that way.

I passed a sign for a pet cemetery this afternoon and I went to see it. It was off the bumpiest dirt road I've ever been on – you'd have been clutching your chest, Martin, yelling about axles and to turn back, oh yes you would. But I was very careful and nothing happened, the car seemed interested in getting there, too. I'd never been to a pet cemetery before. It's a heartbreaking and wonderful experience, the crooked signs, the used toys marking the heads of graves, the animals' names, most of them ending in Y, of course. There was a parakeet named Petey, a cat named Roly Poly. A lot of dogs – Rusty, Tippy, one called Admiral Commander III. I found a little boy, about seven, sitting at the side of one of the graves – his dog Sparky was buried there. Part bulldog, he said, mostly bulldog. The boy, named Ralph, said he never thought Sparky would die – he didn't seem to be that sick, but he never came back from the vet's. He told me Sparky snorted when he laughed, that's what he said, that the dog laughed and that he snorted when he did so. Ralph had his skateboard with him, he visited every day on his rounds. He had a new dog now, Ruffian was his name. But as Ralph so eloquently explained, "Ruffian is his self, but this one here, that's Sparky."

It is rather a luxury to go on this way, Martin, to know that you are attending to what I am saying. That you will read this letter through, perhaps twice, because it is a letter and not me.

I wish you could see this quilt, the stitches so tiny and fine and hand done. But even as I say this, I feel some reservation, a stinginess of spirit. Because I don't think you'd appreciate the stitches. If you'd been driving, I wouldn't even be here.

Not long ago, I saw a woman in a drugstore pick something up in her hand, delighted, and hold it out toward her husband. It was just a perfume bottle, but the shape of it was lovely. "See this, hon?" she said. And the man said, "Yeah," but he had his back to her and was walking down the aisle away from her. The woman put the thing back, diminished.

Do you know what I mean, Martin? I think this comes from mistakes so many women make early on in a marriage. When we got engaged, I stopped driving my own car. I rode shotgun every time we were together. The default settings on the mirrors, on the closeness of the seat to the wheel, they were yours. Remember when that car caught on fire, the engine? Maybe it was auto grief. Don't think I'm crazy, Martin. I have only gotten out my shovel, to dig a bit. I'm just pointing out what I uncover. You can look or not. I want the difference to be that I don't put the thing back on the shelf because you say it's not worth seeing.

I just read this letter over and I see that there is a lot of anger here.

I'm sorry.

Love,
Nan

I am staying at a bed-and-breakfast on the edge of a lake. The windows are wide open and the wind has come in to snoop around, to lift the doilies, to blow up the edges of the bedspread, to push at the closet door, creating a low and urgent rattle. I can hear waves lapping at the shore and the sound is faintly obscene. There is an owl hooting somewhere out there, but I can't see him.

I took a walk earlier, just around the block. The sidewalks heaved crazily, damage from the tree roots below, and at one point I tripped and nearly fell flat on my face. An older man walking behind me came rushing up, asking if I were all right. I said I was fine, thank you. He said, wasn't it a lovely evening? and I said it certainly was. Good weather will do this to people, bond them in their gratefulness. The man was wearing wrinkly clothes and he had prickly looking gray stubble on his face. Cactus man.

He told me he'd been a lifer in the US Army. "Logistics," he said. "Know what that is?" Not exactly, I said. "Well," he said, "it's the most important thing. First ones in, first ones out." Uh-huh, I said. I didn't want to talk army. The sky was a mixed color, peaches and blue. I *wanted to think about that. Or I wanted to think about the fact that this old guy was once my age. He was once younger than I, and I imagined him slicking his hair back to dance in the moonlight with girls whose perfume scent frightened him and aroused him. How different they were, dressed in smashable taffeta, so carefully arranged in hair and in makeup and in words. Everything about them practiced, and he raw and improvising. The pearl of their teeth through the passion of their dark lipstick, should he? The shadowy and too tender indentation at the base of their necks, how could he? We passed a small library and the man said, "I know all the gals in there." I thought, I'll bet he does. I'll bet he comes in regularly, leans on the counter and chats and chats and chats with the "gals" and they chat back, and when they turn away from him they smile at each other with a gentle weariness. I'll bet his name is Willy or something like that, and he puts down beer in the VFW hall in the late afternoons, his hat pushed to the back of his head. I'll bet he has many keys on his key chain and that the fob is tacky and meaningful. Baloney must be in his refrigerator. His socks must be thin and cheap and the blue that turns purple, and he must not be strict about how many days in a row they are put to the task.*

Our steps made such a fine sound on the roller-coaster sidewalks. Our conversation was so light and arbitrary and I felt like my imagination was off the leash and rolling in the grass that had turned bluish in the setting sun.

I still feel that way now, that my imagination is free,

that I have a red carpet unfurled before me like Dorothy's yellow brick road and I can go on and on. Speak, this journal says. I'm listening to you. Go ahead and say anything. Confess. Exult. Weep. Nothing makes me walk away. Nothing bores me. The truth is always interesting, whatever form it takes.

I am washed up and settled in for sleep in a stranger's bed, which always feels luxurious to me. There is something about being handed buttered toast as opposed to making it yourself, and there is something about lying against another person's selection of sheets. Not a hotel's choice, a person's, who had a dialogue in their mind before making their selection. Too many violets? No, I don't think so, and look at the blue next to them, that's nice.

I've been thinking about that waiter Lawrence's house. He did have an amazing amount of angel paraphernalia – calendars, wallpapers, figurines, many pictures, bookmarks, coffee mugs, even a bathroom rug. I'm afraid he was on the way from refreshingly eccentric to fearfully peculiar. Such a slight and delicate thing he was, the waist of a woman dancer, a wrist with skin so translucent I could see the blue lines of his veins like an etching. We had some tea (Celestial Seasonings, of course), and he told me he was a little sad that angels are so popular now, because he'd loved them long ago, from the time he was a little boy; and when too many people love what you do, some of the pleasure is lost. When he was seven, he'd used the shoelaces from his sneakers to anchor an angel figurine at the head *of his bed. Unfortunately it had fallen and given him a black eye.*

He had difficulty holding jobs, and thought perhaps what he'd do next was apply at the dry cleaner. No customer contact required, he said, he'd just work in the back, alone. He thought it would be hard for him to get into trouble there, didn't I agree? and I said yes, that was probably true, and I tried to sound optimistic, but the truth is it tore at my heart a little that such a true and friendly person must keep to himself.

He asked me where I was going and I said I wasn't sure. I said I was a fifty-year-old runaway and he said really! and there was some admiration there and suddenly I felt it for myself.

Today, when I was driving down a small, winding road, I came to an albino squirrel, stopped in the middle of the road. It was frozen in place. I didn't have time to stop but I didn't hit it; it was between the wheels. And I was so relieved and then I thought, well, that was probably purposeful; isn't that interesting; that squirrel has learned that if you don't quite make it across, you just hold still and the cars will go over you. But it bothered me, and about ten miles down the road I felt like going back to see if the squirrel had made it over to the side of the road. My first thought was, you can't do that. You'll waste a good half hour. And then I thought, you can too. And I did go back and I saw the squirrel off to the side of the road, dead. Some car had hit it after all, because it hadn't had the courage to *honor its own correct instinct. And I began to cry because I had this thought about people, that they do this all the time, deny the wise voice inside them telling them the right thing to do because it is different. I remembered once seeing a tea party some little girls had set up outside, mismatched china, decorations of a plucked pansy blossom and a seashell and a shiny penny and a small circle of red berries and a fern, pressed wetly into the wooden table, the damp outline around it a beautiful bonus. They didn't consult the Martha Stewart guide for entertainment and gulp a martini before their guests arrived. They pulled ideas from their hearts and minds about the things that gave them pleasure, and they laid out an offering with loving intent. It was a small Garden of Eden, the occupants making something out of what they saw was theirs. Out of what they truly saw.*

Then I started thinking about what else Martin might have done with his life if he hadn't been a salesman. And I think that once in a very great while he thinks about that too, sits outside at night, alone, wondering, and I know the notion pokes at a soft place in him. He is very successful, but he is embarrassed by what he does, he has told me. He wanted to study astrophysics, but when he was ready to apply to graduate school, he saw that there were so many people around him who knew more than he. Not to be racist, he said, but Jesus, those Chinese guys. Who could compete? On Saturdays, Martin would be on the campus smoking a little dope and playing a lot of Frisbee – mostly with dogs who wore kerchiefs around their necks – and he would see the Chinese guys in his classes coming from the library when it closed and think, No, I don't think it runs so deep in me. He went into business. Put his telescope in the basement next to the TV trays we got for a wedding gift and never use but can't throw out. And then I thought of how his bald spot is growing larger and how he was impotent for the first time in his life not long ago and it made me feel so tender toward him I almost called him. But he would not be at the kitchen table thinking about such things. The conversation would not have worked. When are you coming home? he would have said.

After lunch (a perfect cheeseburger at a dime store in the middle of a real Main Street), I passed by a house that stood all by itself, just at the edge of town. It was a chartreuse color, awful really, but at least different. I saw a woman sitting on the porch, watching her children play in the yard, and I remembered my desire to talk to other women. It occurred to me that I could really do it. Well, I could try. I pulled into the driveway, and the woman shaded her eyes against the sun, looking to see who I was.

"I'm not anyone," I said, getting out of the car. And then, "You don't know me." She didn't say anything. I said I was not a salesperson or a Jehovah's Witness and then she smiled, relaxed. She asked if I were lost. I said sort of. She was awfully young, a pretty woman, her short, dark hairdo and large round eyes reminding me of a chickadee. She wore a sweatshirt and jeans and lovely pearl studs in her ears – dressing up a bit of herself so she wouldn't forget *how, no doubt. You will see this in mothers of small children: they dress up from the neck up. Everything else is in danger of peanut butter.*

I sat down with her – although a step below her out of some sense of propriety – and one of her children, a boy who looked to be around four or so, came running up at full speed, then stopped dead in his tracks before me. I said hello and he said nothing, just looked at his mother. "She's lost," the mother said. "She just needs directions." "Oh," he said, in that kind of adenoidal voice kids often have. Then he ran off to join his slightly younger sister, who was adjusting her doll in the buggy with straight-mouthed determination. The boy faced away from her, made a gun out of a stick, fired into the woods at the enemy. The ancient roles.

I used to play with my cousins in the basement of our grandparents' house. They were the warriors; we girls were the nurses, left to talk quietly to each other and make a hospital from towels we found in the laundry and lawn furniture stored in the cobwebby furnace room. One by one, the boys showed up with whatever wounds they described to us: "My guts are hanging out, right here, see? Pretend it's just all gloppy intestines, real slimy." Or "My bone is sticking out of my arm plus my ear got shot off." Or "I'm dead. You have to wrap me up like a mummy and call my parents." We cared for them, smiling with a kind of bruised superiority, silent.

The young woman asked me if I would like a cup of

*coffee. I said I would love one. She said she'd be right back
and then when she stood up, there was just the tiniest hint
of fear in her, a hesitancy – as though she were thinking.
Wait, should I leave this stranger out here with my
children, should I be getting coffee for someone who might
be a bad headline tomorrow? But I looked at her and smiled
my intentions and this worked; people still often com-
municate best without words. The woman came out with a
yellow mug with blackberries painted on it and we drank
our coffee and I told her about what I was doing. Said I'd
decided I needed a trip away, just by myself, that my
husband was back home, we were fine, I just . . . And she
sighed and said yeah, she loved her husband but that
she ran away from him with some frequency. I said, really?
She said, yes, most of the time he knew nothing about it.
But once he did. They'd had a bad fight late at night and she
took off in the car, meaning never to come back, meaning
to drive to Alaska and begin again. But she was barefoot
and this seemed to prevent her from doing anything. She
said she drove to the grocery store and slept in the parking
lot until three-thirty, then snuck back into the house. "But
I didn't go to bed. I slept on the couch," she said. "I didn't
want him to know I was home." "Right," I said, and I
thought, how can it be that two strangers are exchanging
such intimate things? Well, most women are full to the
brim, that's all. That's what I think. I think we are most of
us ready to explode, especially when our children are small
and we are so weary with the demands for love and*

attention and the kind of service that makes you feel you should be wearing a uniform with "Mommy" embroidered over the left breast, over the heart. I too sat on porches, on park benches, half watching Ruthie and half dreaming – trying, I think, to recall my former self. If a stranger had come up to me and said, "Do you want to talk about it? I have time to listen," I think I might have burst into tears at the relief of it. It wasn't that I was really unhappy. It was the constancy of my load and the awesome importance of it; and it was my isolation. I made no friends out of the few people I saw in the park – frazzled mothers too busy for a real conversation; discontented nannies staring blankly ahead. And oftentimes the park was empty. The swings clanked so loudly against the pole. I could hear Ruthie's little voice carried on the wind toward me, always toward me. Watching her small back bent over her bucket in the sandbox, I ached with love for her and fingered the pages of the novel I couldn't really read. I watched the time, because I had to have dinner ready when Martin came home. It was a rule neither of us ever thought to question or unmake. We flowered in the sixties, but the spirit of the fifties was deep in us. We saw what our parents did, and, blinking blandly like the baby chimps in the jungle, followed suit – at first in ways that felt clumsy, then in ways we called natural, though in me, I see now, there were internal earthquakes wanting to happen all the time.

I asked the woman how she was doing, how did she really think she was doing. "Oh," she said. "Fine. Although

. . . well, I know this is just temporary. But yesterday I shook the orange juice and the top was loose and a little bit spilled on the floor which I'd already wiped up about three hundred times that day and I just started crying. I went to sit in the bathroom, but of course I had to leave the door cracked open. I'll bet I cried for twenty minutes. In the middle of it, I got my daughter a graham cracker. She didn't notice a thing." I said, but you believe you're all right, that you're doing fine? Well, yes, she said. Sure.

I drove the rest of the day feeling that my mind was wrapped in a blanket, insulated. I noted what I passed as though it were in someone else's dream. I came back into myself after dinner, which was in a truck stop. There was a special area for "professional drivers" to eat where the service was extra fast. The room was filled with smoke, a blue haze. I saw one woman there – the rest were men. The menu posted over the counter was full of things that the American Heart Association would have had a collective heart attack about, and everybody there was eating them with gusto. I myself had chicken-fried steak, in the other room, the one for civilians. We didn't get phones at our booths. We didn't get shower services – I kept hearing over the intercom, "Roadway, your shower is ready. Carolina, your shower is ready." I asked for a little extra gravy and the waitress brought it to me in a soup bowl. There are places time doesn't touch, I guess.

There was a store there, too, a kind of 7-Eleven for 18-wheelers, attached right to the restaurant. They had an *amazing variety of junk food, including the biggest bag of the biggest pieces of beef jerky I ever saw; strange pieces of black or silver metal equipment that I couldn't begin to identify; sheepskin seat covers; shellacked wooden plaques with "Prayer for a Trucker" written on them and featuring an illustration of an angel hovering over a truck as it made its way down a mountain road in a blizzard (if I'd known Lawrence's address, I'd have sent him one). There was a whole rack full of black leather jackets, and, for the ladies, lace-trimmed, sleeveless T-shirts with a picture of a motorcycle done in pink and blue pastels. I bought one, couldn't stop myself from smiling when I walked out with it. Do you want this? life seems to be saying. Is this what you want? Well, take it, then. What do you think it's here for?*

It feels like this is my time for coming into my own. Extraordinary to suddenly think of this as a time for gain. Martin used to say, imitating his funny old grandmother, "Oy, I can't vait to get home and take my goidle off." Well, my girdle's off. Flung into the wind. What luxury, the feel of one's true flesh beneath one's own hand.

Dear Martin,

I am at a booth in a diner, and I just ordered your favorite breakfast: two over easy, sausage, home fries, wheat toast. As you know, I don't like sausage as much as bacon, but I am doing this in honor of you. Well, not in honor of you. In remembrance of you. Because I kind of miss you.

I didn't sleep much last night, and so I have that fragile kind of feeling. You know how I get when I'm tired, when any negative thing can seem to poke a hole right through me – a newspaper headline, running out of Kleenex, the messiness of a little girl's braids. You know how I get. I think it's something you were always very patient about, really, and I don't think I ever thanked you for it.

Well, the waitress just brought the coffee and I must say it is the best I've ever had – caramel-colored from the real cream, a slight taste of pecan that makes you almost want to chew. This diner is called the Metro. Not many people are here right now, and you can hear bits of conversation. Two old guys in the corner, their pants hiked up to their armpits, are talking about their blood pressure medication – "Doc told me I could *expect* that, but hell, who *needs* it?" one of them is saying, with the tremulous kind of outrage that is soft at the center, that breaks your heart. Even as I approach old age, I can't stop looking at older people and assuming they were never young. Whereas they can't believe they are now old. One of my grandmothers used to say, "I wake up every morning and look in the mirror to see if I've started to go backward yet. I never have." And then she said to me, quite seriously, "Darling. Don't get old."

In a booth at the other end of the room are two young mothers, their babies in strollers beside them. I'll bet they're talking about their husbands. Do men ever do that, Martin? Talk about their wives at some length? Try to figure them out?

Before my eggs arrive I want to tell you what I did last night. I spent the whole day doing not much more than driving. I passed so many lovely things – a wide brook that followed alongside the road and made a wonderful sound – I turned off the radio to hear it. There was a long patch of woods with DO NOT ENTER signs all over the place, and I confess it made me want to ENTER. I miss being young and rebellious. I wish I'd gone to more protest rallies. Remember when everyone was going to Washington that time? It was before I was with you. My current flame, a wild-eyed artist named Chico, came to get me to go, but I said no, I was too tired. I said I was too tired! I thought my whole life would be one opportunity after the other to make important statements.

Chico painted on huge canvases, often with his feet. He swam naked in a pond that was behind his crooked house, and it always pissed him off that I wore a bathing suit when I went in. He had a rowboat, and once when we were out in it he dove in the water and took the boat's rope in his teeth and swam me back to shore. I suppose I was meant to be impressed or something but I was just annoyed. He gave me crabs, Chico. I was so embarrassed to have them. I remember when I told you, years later, that I'd had them – I thought you should know – and you said, so what? Everybody had them. I said did you? and you said sure, that you and your roommates used to have races with them across the lid of the toilet seat.

Not that you really need to know this, but my eggs are here. More later.

Well, I'm through with a delicious breakfast where the home fries were *not* made from canned potatoes, and the waitress has just said, Sit here as long as you want, honey, take your time, tell me when you don't want any more coffee. So I will finish this letter to you. Someone has put Hank Williams Junior on the jukebox, and I am feeling quite content. The coffee has given me enough of a charge that I want all my *i*'s to be dotted, this paper to be folded exactly into thirds before it gets put in the envelope.

So. As I was saying, I saw lots of wonderful things – fields plowed in ways that were so neat and orderly, and farmhouses set back from the road, the kind that always make me think the occupants eat at tables with blue-and-white dishes, embroidered tablecloths, jelly glasses that are sparkling clean. Cows stood in pastures like chess pieces, rarely moving, seeming to contemplate some unhysterical thing. I passed several houses in one town with quilts over the railings, out for an airing – quilting must be big, there. I was not thinking about much of anything, just driving and looking, driving and looking. When I ate dinner, there was a man sitting across from me reading a paperback that had a cover of a night sky. And it made me think about how I've always been so afraid of the dark, how I get a kind of claustrophobia when I am alone in the dark. I feel something surrounding me, kind of squeezing, and I wait for something awful to happen. It's like hearing an evil mind thinking, and then the thoughts gain form and reach out toward you. And you are immobilized by your own too-strong desire to get away. My mouth gets dry, my heart beats so hard. I hate this about myself. I'm fifty years old and I still leave the hall light on when you're out of town – as well as a light in every room downstairs. Looking at that book cover, I thought, Well, this is my time of discovery, this trip. This is my time to let new things happen, and to enter into fears in order to come out the other side. And so I bought a sleeping bag – not the kind you would have bought, I know; you would have researched sleeping bags and bought the most sensible one, and after you bought it you would have researched still, making sure you got the best price – whereas I simply went into a store and bought the one I thought was prettiest. And least complicated – my God, Martin, some of them seem like they ought to enter themselves in a talent contest. I drove until I came to a heavily wooded area, and then I pulled over to the side of the road and walked in a way. The sun was setting – it was so quiet, no birds, no squirrels, nothing but the sound of my steps breaking twigs. It felt like *On the Beach*, like the world had died and I was the sole witness. I laid the sleeping bag out and got into it, and when the dark came, I was just petrified. I thought, this is how it happens. People go too far, they get foolish, and they get killed.

Still, it seemed very, very important that I do this, that I confront this fear of the dark, access my woman warrior – don't smile, Martin, it is in us all, we are just well-behaved, and for all of humankind men have reaped the benefits of the first woman who said for the very first time, "That's all right. You can go first." Anyway, I thought, if I can just stay alone one night, I won't be afraid anymore.

I stayed the whole night. And I must say it was the longest night of my life. I closed my eyes and tried to sleep but there was no way I was going to have the kind of trust that would let me stop jumping at every breeze, every buzz of every mosquito (and there were many). When the sun came up, I burst into tears. Then I walked back to the car and got in and locked the doors and I drove to the gas station and washed up and put on deodorant and perfume and lipstick and a gold bracelet that was at the bottom of my purse. I guess it wasn't exactly a vision quest. I guess it was just a woman trying not to be afraid of the dark, who still is.

One thing I want to tell you about all this is that the fear I felt lying alone in the dark was close to the anxiety I feel when I wake up at home. That sense of something out there that has no respect for my life. With the exception of my night in the woods, since I've been on the road, those middle-of-the-night panics have not been happening. I wake up and think about where I am, I lie awake for a while, but I am not afraid. I am just – well, I don't know how to say this to you. I am just realizing. I guess that's what I'd say.

Watch out when you pay the milkman. The last three times he charged for cottage cheese which I never ordered.

Love,
Nan

I spent the night in the woods last night. I wanted to end up feeling calm and safe and a part of the orbiting earth. This was a romantic and completely unrealistic notion. I ended up feeling like a tidbit being dangled over the jaws of a wolf. I was so afraid the whole night, stiff with fear, literally afraid to move. Now it is five o'clock in the evening and I am in a filthy motel, but I don't care. I only need sleep, and this will do for that. I don't think I've ever gone to bed so early in my life. It feels very odd, yet very comforting, too, turning to pajamas in my time of need.

I will write for a while, then sleep as long as I want to.

I tried saying the rosary last night, to calm myself, but it had no effect. So I tried to remember every lover I'd ever had. This was a very interesting thing that did not lessen my fright but at least kept my mind occupied. Martin and I once did this, sat at the kitchen table and tried to write down the name of every person we'd ever slept with. It was my idea, of course. I thought that it would . . . well, I don't really know what I thought it would do. Maybe I just wanted to know. Anyway, my list was longer, which surprised me. Men's wrists should be bigger than women's, and men's lists of lovers should be longer, I guess that's what I believed. We told each other about all our lovers, too, which we had never done before. We were very careful to paint them all in an unflattering light of some kind or another. Every story about every person ended up with some unfortunate inclusion – my favorite was Martin telling me that one woman snorted the first time he made love to her and he just couldn't stand her after that. He demonstrated, snorted lightly in a rapid, rhythmic way and we both laughed. It was, in a way, a very good experience, but we didn't tell the whole truth, I know we didn't.

You are where I unlock myself, where I say that I have often put down my wooden spoon to stare at the kitchen window to see the men I thought were magic for their story-telling or their way of walking, or the ones I was so strongly sexually attracted to, even though they weren't good people – at least not for me.

There is one thing I never told Martin about. When I was in high school, I met a twenty-five-year-old man who said he would teach me everything I needed to know about sex – without actually having sex with me. You can be a pre-bed student, he said, winking. I was at a burger place with a girlfriend of mine, she'd introduced me to this man, Joey was his name. She had dated him, she always dated older men. He was obviously not the brightest guy in the world, but he was very handsome. I had a reputation – entirely deserved – for being extremely naïve sexually. I got teased a lot and I was tired of it. I was off to college in the fall; I wanted to know something when I got there. On senior skip day, I told my mother I was going swimming with my class, but I went instead to meet this man, who was going to take me to a motel.

Isn't it funny, I fell asleep last night after I wrote the above, the pen in my hand. I woke up around four, put you on the bedside table, got a drink, and went back to bed. But you, open to this page, felt to me like a spectator dressed in black. A silent presence standing too near, crowding me. I closed you, moved you to the bathroom floor, then shut the door so that I could not hear you calling.

I never told Martin about this event, and I never told myself, either. I realize that, now. I realize that's why I went to sleep, because years away from it, I still don't want to face it. But I'm going to, here. Sometimes night is outside you; sometimes it is in you.

I still feel a kind of fear. An awful shame. I went to a lecture once by a famous psychiatrist who was talking about how women must rid themselves of the idea that they are sitting on the ground, eyes cast downward, waiting for a man to tap them on the shoulder. It is a very common feeling, I know. When he said that, the woman sitting next to me recrossed her legs and straightened herself in her seat, the truth of what he said snaking through her, through all of us there. The air in the room seemed to change, to become charged and visible. What he did not say is how the story repeats itself over and over, how once a woman is tapped, she is likely to get up and do what she is bid, then sit down and wait again. Where does this start, I want to know? When do we leave behind staring straight at someone, not worrying if, in the middle of the conversation, there's a mosquito bite we need to scratch?

I believed, at twelve, that I could be a scientist. I read a book a day. I believed I could be a writer, an actress, a professor of English in Rome, an acrobat in a purple spangled outfit. Days opened for me like the pulling apart of curtains at a play you've been dying to see. I had a microscope on my desk, shelves full of books and treasures that I found outside: rocks, wood, abandoned nests of hornets and birds, notes to myself for things to do tomorrow because I hadn't had the time today. I believed the way to ride bareback was to get on and go, the rising heat of the horse against your bare legs the only instruction you'd need. The how of everything was simply in the doing of it. I had a turtle in a plastic bowl, and I fed him flies I captured with my bare hands and to whom I apologized before killing. I had a crow living outside my window, I spoke to all the dogs in the neighborhood, and they understood me. I patted them so hard dust rose up off their backs in tiny, dim clouds, and they understood this, too – they stood still for it for as long as I would do it, their eyes closed in itchy pleasure. My life was like a wild, beating thing, exotic, capable of unfolding and enlarging itself, pulling itself higher and higher up like a kite loved by the wind, and it was captured beneath my cereal bowl.

There in front of me, my own for the taking. And then, suddenly, lost.

And look, now, how I avoid this still. How I use my own hand to turn my face away.

Here. I will say it all now. No stopping. Like a dive into the deep end, intent on making it to the shallow end without surfacing.

I took a bus to the motel. I still remember the driver, he wore a gray cardigan sweater with brown leather buttons, and his resemblance to my beloved grandfather was so strong that I nearly turned around to go home. But I didn't. I got on the bus, sat alone in a seat by the window, feeling as though I were being pulled somewhere by an uncaring hand. Feeling also that although I had chosen this, I had not really had a choice. There was a mother sitting across from me with twins, toddlers, and I stared at them the whole time, wanting the mother to pull me into her watchful circle, to say, "Oh, honey. Don't do that. Come with us." I thought of how everyone else at school was going swimming, how later they'd have a big picnic, and there would be no gap left anywhere for me.

The bus got to the stop where Joey and I had agreed to meet, somewhere near the motel, and I saw his car, the engine running, his hand out the window holding a cigarette. I got off the bus and he opened his car door, stepped out, waved at me. I waved back with one hand, pressed the other hard into my own middle. I was thinking, well, his real name is Joseph. And he was on time, he likes me. When I got in the car, he told me to lie down on the floor until he said it was all right to get up. He said no one should see me or we'd get in a lot of trouble. I lay on the floor trying to keep my sweater from getting dirty – it was a light pink, angora; and I was wearing a gray straight skirt with it, new nylons, and my black flats that I'd polished the night before. I had a barrette with pearls on it anchored to one side of my hair. When I put it in, I had imagined him taking it out, my hair falling to my shoulders in a way I thought he might admire. I thought he might touch my curls, gently, hold one strand of hair up to the light to see better the reddish color it could take on. I'd thought he might kiss my hair, then my neck, and then my lips. Now I could only see his shoes, his foot working the gas pedal and the brake with some impatience. I thought, I don't know those shoes at all. I could hear his keys in the ignition jingling softly against one another and I wondered why he had so many keys. It seemed dangerous to me, that he would have so many keys. He stopped the car, told me he was going into the office to get a room, and not to move "Okay," I said, and my voice was so high and strange. And I remember I looked at each of my fingernails when I waited for him, because I wanted him to think every part of me was pretty. I'd painted my nails pearl pink the night before. I'd put perfume in places I'd never put it before.

Well, I am just shaking! Perhaps there is no point in remembering this. I don't think there is any reason. It was

*a very bad experience, over now. I am fifty. It is over,
now.*

*All right. I will say the worst part. Let me do that. Then it
will be over.*

There was a point at which he was straddling me, we
were both naked, my God, I had never been naked with
anyone before, not even partially, except for the ancient
doctor I went to, and he had the sensitivity to look at the
wall when he put his hands to me under the paper gown.
But Joey looked directly at me and he put his penis on my
chest and pushed my breasts together hard. Then he rubbed
himself between them. "Doesn't this feel nice?" he said, his
voice hoarse, close to cruel. He was so far above me. If I
looked up, I could see the inside of his nose, which seemed
too intimate, and which seemed rude for me to do. Anyway,
I didn't want to look at him, it embarrassed me to do that.
I'd caught a glimpse of his penis and the fleshy sight of it
made me feel like vomiting. I didn't know where to look.
The wallpaper was peeling, the lamp buzzed, the door to
the bathroom was cracked open, and I could hear the drip
of the faucet. I closed my eyes and tried not to cry. I could
see my bed at home, my heart-shaped pillow lying against
the other pillows. And then he put his hand to my face and
opened my mouth. "Don't bite," he said, and he was
laughing a little, and then he was not, and the bed squeaked
and squeaked and squeaked. The barrette had slipped to the
back of my head and it pressed into me, and I felt I could

not move to adjust it. It ended up making a small wound
that kept me tender for a long time.

Why tell more? The silent ride home? The way he
barely looked at me when we said good-bye?

I am exhausted again. I am going to sleep until I wake
up far away from this place I've been to.

Dear Martin,

Today, around noontime, I suddenly got tired of the car. And so when I came to the next town, I pulled over and parked next to a church and got out to take a little walk. It was a small town, the requisite town hall and police station and library all clustered together like gossiping friends. I sat on the steps of the town hall eating an ice cream and trying to decide which direction to go in. I could see some railroad tracks off in the distance and I decided to walk along there.

I'd forgotten all the pleasures of walking in a place like that – the low twist of anxiety about a train coming when you're in a narrow spot, the crunch of gravel alongside the tracks, the splintery wooden slats beneath the rusty silver rail, the rare wildflower in among the weeds, bowing to the breezes. I passed an old gentleman also out walking, and we stopped to chat for a while. He was well into his seventies, perhaps even his eighties, and still good-looking, you didn't have to stretch to say so. He wore a green plaid shirt tucked into khaki pants, a braided belt, a pair of ultramodern sneakers. He said he lived in a nearby retirement center, and needed to get out and walk daily to get away from the girls. "No offense," he said, "but they get to be like horseflies. Oh, I like them, like to sit and play cards with them in the evening, they're all wearing their sparkly earrings and such, but all *day* . . ." He said the ratio of women to men in the place was 11:1. I asked him how long he'd lived there and he said seven years, ever since his wife, Honey, died. "That wasn't her real name," he said. "Eleanor was her real name. But I never called her anything but Honey. It fit her, she thought so, too." They had nine children, and all of them are still close. One of his sons worked at NASA, one daughter studied opera in New York, the rest were just normal, nice people, he said – Americans, he said. He asked how many children I had and I said one; and you know, Martin, I suddenly felt ashamed that we only had one. As though we were dabbling in family, not really serious. He asked where I lived and I said outside of Boston and he said oh, far from home, was I visiting? I said no, just . . . traveling. He said, well if I were there at dinnertime not to miss Randy's Lunch, right downtown, best damned meatloaf in the state. He said he went and snuck a bite every now and then even though if his doctor knew, he'd have his head. "It's not going to hurt me," he said, leaning close, as though his doctor might have a microphone planted in the tree nearby. "I swear to God it's what's keeping me alive at this point." He had dimples like yours, Martin, deep ones on either side of his face.

Do you know that you're still handsome? When you look into the mirror, do you feel a tug of the old satisfaction? I've noticed I don't look in the mirror much at all anymore. I used to be quite vain, I know. But it's been a while since I turned any heads. This has been kind of hard for me. I never liked it when it was happening, it made me so nervous, used to be I couldn't sit in a restaurant without knowing someone was watching me eat, well not just me, of course, men in restaurants gaze on the good-looking women, staring first at this one, then at that one. Staring and making up their little scenes, we can feel them doing it. But now I am seen by men as a number in line, a bakery customer; some old gal who needs her sink fixed; the driver of the nice Mercedes passing through a road-construction site. I feel this loss in a kind of vague way, I guess it's not so bad, what was I going to do, become a Mrs Robinson? Still, it's odd to lose the power, this thing that lets you have a little something happen with every man you come in contact with. If you are a pretty woman, you get favors, and I was pretty. Not the gorgeous kind of pretty that makes men nervous and often angry, just the calm kind of pretty that makes men be a little kinder, rub with some sensuality the keys in their pockets, occasionally have ideas they mostly keep to themselves. Although Charlie Benderman, did I ever tell you what he whispered to me at the Maxwells' Christmas party? No, I didn't tell you. Well, he thought we should see how heavy the guests' coats felt if we were under them, if you know what I mean. Do you know what I said? I said, "I love my husband, Charlie." And he got all embarrassed and went to freshen his drink. When I watched him walk away, I confess I thought about it, thought about what it might have been like. Tried to remember what underwear I was wearing, if it matched. Wondered what he kissed like.

What I miss acutely is my periods. The last one was so long ago. I guess that was it, I guess I'm done with all that now. It feels so awful. Is that funny to you, Martin, after all the times you heard me complain about my periods? I know, I know, now you're feeling a little nervous, thinking, ah jeez, here we go, Nan's off on another tangent, talking about her periods, for Christ's sake, and I'm supposed to be interested. Could you be interested, though, Martin? Could you try to be? Could you put your load of man stuff aside and just open yourself to hearing about this? It's big as a boulder in me. It's important.

You wait for your period. For what seems like years. You get the pastel-blue booklet with the white rose on the cover and the lecture from which the boys are barred; you are aware that when it comes, when it comes, when it comes, you will be a WOMAN by virtue of the fact that your body, the one that yesterday swung from the monkey bars, can today have a baby. Can grow and deliver to the world a live human being. You know that hormones will course through you, whispering commands; that the pull of the moon will be shared by you and the ocean and the minds of wild things. When your period comes, you prize the mess. You examine the stain, try to read it. You touch the blood, rub it between your fingers. You say to yourself, I am forever changed. Changed. Forever. Well, I did, anyway. The day my period came, I walked down the steps on new legs and showed my mother my underwear as she sat on the sofa, sewing. "Well," she said, blushing, "well, now." She was shy about it, and she turned me away from her to head me upstairs to the linen closet. "You'll need this," she said, not looking at me, "and this." She was leaning into the closet, her apron hanging away from her housedress, and her housedress fallen away from her chest, and I saw her freckled breasts in her old yellow-white brassiere and they looked old and superfluous to me and I felt sorry for her, so far away from my new beginning, my start, my star-spangled life now dropped before me.

When Ruthie got her period, I think it was a better experience for her. I know we smiled right at each other, and I bought her a little pearl necklace to celebrate when we went out to lunch – it was a Saturday, clear blue sky and the kind of sunlight that felt so perfect it seemed fake. We had a nice time, and she asked me not to tell you until the next day, and I didn't. I lay in bed that night feeling the tie between Ruthie and me grow stronger, grow leaves.

What is comparable for you, Martin? Would you tell me if something were? Do you know how much I long for you to lift the rock, to tell me about your underside? You once said, "Women are all the time asking what men are thinking about. We're not thinking about *anything*!" Well, maybe that's true. But we are. We are thinking about things. It seems to me that the working minds and hearts of women are just so interesting, so full of color and life. And one of the most tragic things I've seen is the way that's been overlooked, the way that if you try to discover what the women were doing at any given time in history, you are hard-pressed to find out. Why? I want to say to you that we are not silly, that what we think about and what drives us to talk, talk, talk, this is vital.

Does this follow anything? I mean, is there a particular reason that I bring it up now? I don't know. But I want to say it to you. And I want to say that I don't want to live in our house anymore. I want to move. With you. To the place I pick this time. I have ideas. I've dreamed about the house I want. Next letter, I'll tell you about it.

Love,
Nan

I am in a Hilton hotel in Des Moines. It was time for a little city. I took a Jacuzzi and I went down and had my nails done and I sat at the bar until the silliness drove me back up to my room. I have been sitting on the edge of the bed thinking about what I wrote in here last time. I think every woman I know has a story like that, some incident of paralyzed humiliation involving a man and sex. I'll bet if you asked any woman, was there ever a time when you . . . Oh yes, they'd say. There was this one time . . . My best friend in college told me that she once watched her fraternity boyfriend spray semen around the house, holding his penis in his hands like a fire hose. And she lay in bed, one leg pulled up prettily, genuinely confused, thinking, is this what it's supposed to be? Where is the romance? At least she wasn't frightened.

I visited a trailer park today. I turned down the gravel road, drove slowly, looking at the way the trailers were all decorated: curtains, little picket fences protecting a line of garden, an attempt at a patio under an awning. So many of them seemed so desperate to look as though they weren't trailers at all. And I wondered why those people just didn't get a co-op, some nice little place that didn't have wheels. There was a woman about my age outside hanging washing on a miniature clothesline. I pulled up, got out and introduced myself, said I was just having a look around. Go right ahead, she said, you can look at my spot all you want. She was one of those tough-but-kind people, hard line of black eye makeup, smoker's breath, a fondness for hair spray – and a need, too, what with the severe French twist she wore. She had a pretty spectacular figure, if everything I saw was real. She was wearing silver backless heels, those tight black stretchy pants that look like a second skin, a short-sleeved blue sweater, large silver hoop earrings. She hiked her empty pink basket up against her hip, asked if I were considering living here. I said yes I was. She told me it was a quiet place, there was a duck pond down in the middle of their little private park, a Laundromat on site, though the dryer was pretty regularly out of order. Uh-huh, I said. Grocery store just a mile and a half down the road, she said, King Savings, great beef but stay away from their chicken. Oh, I said, uh-huh. And then she said, "You're not really looking to live here, are you?" I said well, no, probably not. She said she didn't think so, said I didn't look the type. I said is that right. She chuckled and then coughed a few times into her fist, bad smoker's cough. Then she said yeah, that was damn right, laughed again. She was looking off to the side like she was sharing the joke with an invisible ally. I said what type did I look like and she said I looked like the type that went down and volunteered at some suicide prevention center in order to save my own life. Handed over my Joan and Davids to the Goodwill with a sense of regret that they would not be recognized as the great shoes they were. I stood stock-still for a minute, trying to figure this out, because it was so surprising, and because although it was pretty nasty, it was said in such a friendly way. I thought, where did this woman come from? How did she end up here?

She lit a cigarette and offered me one, and though I don't smoke, I took one. Salem. An awful mix of foul and mint. I had a sudden urge to get my hair dyed platinum.

We sat at her little picnic table and she said, Not much of a smoker either, are you, Nan? I said no, but that I'd always wanted to be, that it always looked pretty good to me, sexy, too. She said it was sexy, watch this, and she French-inhaled while she stared me straight in the eye.

Then all of a sudden I asked her, I said, what did you want to do? Oh hell, she said, and stared off into the distance. Then, looking back at me, "Everything." I asked her name and she said Susan Littletree and I said is that your married name and she said yes; and no, her husband was not Native American. What he was, was gone. I said well. She said you'd like to see inside the trailer, wouldn't you? I said yes, I would. She said come ahead, but don't get freaked out at the statues of Mary, it's just a joke. Then, looking over her shoulder as she climbed the steps up, No offense if you're a Mary fan. A believer, one of them. More power to you if you are, she said. You got something.

It was amazing how when you got in that trailer, it seemed like a house. It was clean in there, which surprised me – I'd expected dirty dishes all over, newspapers on the floor. She gave me a tour, showed me her blue bedroom – flowered wallpaper, pink sweetheart roses in a vase at the bedside, along with six or seven Mary statues. The bathroom had gold fixtures, and a magazine rack discreetly off to the side, I saw Bon Appétit in there. She had burnt-orange kitchen counters, dark wooden cabinets, a little window over the sink with white ruffled curtains. There was a booth to eat in, striped brown and white fabric. She looked at her watch, asked me would I like a tuna sandwich, it was close enough to dinnertime. I said I would, but to let me help make it, and I stood at her tiny counter chopping celery and sweet pickles and hard-boiled eggs while she mixed the tuna with the mayonnaise. I was so glad it was Hellmann's, the real thing, none of that mincing fake stuff that you always try so hard to pretend is fine, even though your taste alarm is going berserk.

I said it was awfully nice of her, me just showing up and her offering me a meal. Oh well, she said, she'd always thought that was the way it should be, some people wandering around and other people taking care of them, think of Jesus. I said pardon me? and she said think of Jesus, how he wandered around and people fed him. Washed his feet, too, I said. Come to a bad end, though, didn't he, she said, and I'm afraid we started laughing, which made me feel badly and also a little superstitious because if there is all that heaven and hell and accounting stuff, God was shaking his head.

We sat at her table for a while after we ate and she told me her husband had left her three years ago, took off with her best friend. Susan sold their house and bought this trailer, thinking she'd live here a little while, then move on. Only she hadn't left yet. She worked as a receptionist at a car dealership, got hit on by the salesmen, brought one home occasionally, kicked him out the next morning or even that same night, depending on his level of skill and/or his marital status. She'd heard that Trudy, the woman her husband ran off with, had gotten ovarian cancer. I said that must feel very odd, that probably she felt a weird kind of pity, a reluctant, confused kind; and she said no, she felt a full-blown pity, nothing confused about it, she felt a terrible sadness about the whole damn thing. "I'd go down there and take care of her if she asked me to," she said. "It's for sure he ain't gonna do it right. She'll see that, if she hasn't already. 'Where's my dinner?' he'll be saying. 'What, you can't even make dinner?'"

We went shopping, drove over to a huge mall. I told her I wanted to buy her something. She said all right. We looked at all kinds of things, and she settled on a turquoise nightgown and matching robe, on sale, and a new potato peeler. That was all she'd let me get her. I got a few books, a new pair of shoes – she'd got me going with that talk about Joan and Davids. I liked her so much, everything about her, and at one point I asked if she'd like to come *along for a while, that I'd pay her way back home from any place we got to. She said well where was I going? I said nowhere. Anywhere. I was just going around, seeing. She thought about it, then said, hell, she couldn't leave, she'd lose her damn job. I said oh, you can get another one, jobs like that are easy to get. And she cooled then, looked me in the eye, said, you don't know a thing about it, Nan.*

I took her home, then drove another fifty miles in the dark, thinking oh well, it probably wouldn't have worked out anyway, thinking that the purpose of this trip was to spend a lot of time alone, not to start insulating myself from all I might see. The radio was playing a lot of old songs, Frank Sinatra when he was skinny, Tony Bennett, Patti Page. It's good to be in a car, the dark around you, when songs like that are on. I'm getting used to driving so much. Seems like it's part of me, now. I wake up and think, Go.

I know my own luck. I know how rare it is for a person to be able to do this. And I know more and more what I'm doing it for. I feel a kind of strength starting to happen that is wholly legitimate, that is not some trapping I wear until it falls off. It is as though the thing has roots, and seeks the sun with its face turned toward it. And I know I never would have found it without leaving.

Once I took a job on the community newspaper, writing a weekly column. "Nan's Notes on Life," it was called, silly. Well, no it was not. The editor there, a nice woman, told me I had real talent. I told Martin and he said, "Who said that?" I told him, and he said, "Oh." And the bottom fell out. What I am seeing now is that it never was up to him. He could have been more generous. He could have been sensitive. But how I felt, that was not up to him. I only let it be. No more. Perhaps it will be a relief for him not to have to decide for me how I feel. I should think it would be.

For now, the pleasure of heavy blankets and cream-colored sheets, a room-service menu that I intend to study for the best choice in breakfasts. Tomorrow I will make the twin cities of St Paul and Minneapolis.

I am so much farther away than I thought I'd go.

Dear Ruthie,

I don't think I'll be able to express just how much our conversation tonight meant to me. You have no idea how frightened I was to call you, how ready I was for accusations, protestations, questions that I could not answer with any grace or even any legitimacy. But you were so – well, I don't even know the word for it. Calm. Unsurprised. Supportive. Interested. Thank you, Ruthie.

I'm glad you're checking in on Dad. He pretends to not need much, but he does. Don't worry about him eating the same thing every night. This is what he does when I go away. When I went to Aunt Bernice's funeral and stayed with Grandma for a week, I found a stack of Hungry Man frozen-dinner cartons in the garbage when I got home. He'd eaten the same kind every night, I think he likes the Salisbury steak, in fact I think he eats two of them at a time. He's all right in that department. What he needs is a kind of reassurance. We are what he checks himself against, you and I. So if you call every few days and just let him talk, that would be nice. He'll tell you about his job and so on, just let him go and then tell him you'll be calling back soon. He'll be fine. He has a bit of a relationship with the neighbors, he likes to go out and inspect his lawn and chat with them for a bit while he has his evening coffee, oftentimes he likes to drive to the Dunkin' Donuts to get it, they know him there, and he takes a particular kind of pride in that. "Don't even say my order," he says. "I walk in and they pour it up." And of course he has his television shows. I'm writing him every day, as he told you. I'm glad he's saving the letters.

I'll be in Minnesota tomorrow. We've never been there. I hear the people are very friendly. I'll let you know. I will let you know everything I can, Ruthie. Isn't it funny, the two of us thinking so much about the same thing all this time, and neither of us saying much about it.

All your life, Ruthie, when I thought about you, I thought, oh, this is her best time. But then I kept changing my mind, thinking, no, *now* is her best time. And here it is, happening again.

You are always in my thoughts. When you were little, I knew your whereabouts at any given moment. Now that you are a young woman and off on your own, I still always know where you are, because I keep you in my heart. Don't give me your don't-be-so-mushy lecture. It won't do a bit of good.

When I come home, let's make everything we love

and eat it all at once. It will be even better than that pie party we had. I still remember that, do you? You were six, and you and I stood at the head of a long, long table we'd rented that was just covered with pies. My God, it was an extraordinary sight. It was beautiful. Forty-seven guests, all showing up with their favorites, some people with two kinds, they couldn't decide what to make. Theresa Zinz made the best lemon meringue pie I ever tasted, nothing I've had since has ever come close, people were buzzing around her like bees, but she wouldn't part with the recipe, which frankly I thought was small-minded. But poor Ida Young, nobody wanted her rum raisin but her. I remember thinking, what a fabulous idea you'd had, just . . . pie. You should hold that close, Ruthie. You should never lose that, that sense that an impulse can become a real thing.

Watch *Nightline* with Dad if you decide to come home for a visit. You won't hear a word Ted Koppel says, because Dad will be talking over him the whole time, setting him straight. But it's a comfort to your father to have someone listen to him, suggesting by their silence that what he says is true.

I'm buying souvenirs for both of you. I got Dad a pair of moccasins with Corvettes beaded on to the fronts. Very attractive. They'll go well with the Dopey T-shirt you brought him back from Disneyland. He wears that shirt every time it's clean, wears it to bed, did you know?

I'll call you again, soon. It's nice to know you're there, Ruthie. Always has been.

Love,
Mom

Dear Martin,

Today as I drove, a patch of sun lay against my throat. At first it felt warm and comforting; then it began to feel too hot. There was no way for me to adjust the visor to block the light, so I put my hand there, and it got hot, too. And I thought of Sam Kearny, you remember how he had to get radiation to his throat? and I wondered if it burned him and then I thought, I hope I don't have to get that. Sometimes when I wake up at night it's to do an inventory of what might happen, how I might go. This is not just a function of my age, I know; it used to happen with some regularity when I was in my mid-twenties, not too long after Ruthie was born. I'd wake up and think, "But wait. This won't last. I'll have to die." I think it was because Ruthie was so important, and I wanted to stay forever to make sure she was all right forever.

Back then, when I had those anxious nights, I used to get up very carefully so as not to wake you, and go to watch Ruthie sleep. She was so little then, not even two, still in a crib, and she slept with her butt up in the air, her arm around her bedraggled Doggie. I would hear her soft breathing, see the dim outline of her toys scattered around her room. The white rocker I'd nursed her in was still in the corner, the curtains I'd made her were hanging there, just as they did in the daytime. Being in her room always worked to calm me down. I would cover her again – her blanket was always off her – and pick up one of her toys, sit in the rocker with it, move back and forth in the ancient rhythm. I would think, tomorrow I will give her some ABC soup for lunch in her blue bowl, and I'll give her little squares of toast with it; and for dessert, some vanilla yogurt with strawberries sliced on top. After her nap, we will walk to the library and look for birds' nests in the bushes – she liked to find them, she always asked was there a mommy *and* a daddy that lived there, and this always made me think, I can never get a divorce. Not that I thought about it so much then. I did think about it later, though I only told you about it once. Do you remember that morning? Ruthie was eight years old, off to school, and you were leaving for work in one of the suits you'd just bought – a very nice Italian silk, I remember it was a wonderful taupe color with a minute pattern, your cologne was fabulous – and I was sitting in the chair in my bathrobe with my terrible coffee breath and I said to you, Martin, I'm too lonely. And you said, Oh Jesus, Nan, not now. I said, Martin, I need romance. And you said, So have an affair. I looked up at you and I said, You bastard, I want a divorce. And you looked at your watch, and I really think if I'd had a gun I would have shot you. You said you had to go, you were late, we'd talk that night, but we didn't.

You never knew this, but the reason we didn't talk is that I went to lunch with one of my old girlfriends that day and she told me how much trouble she was having with her husband. By comparison, we seemed great. I remember that after lunch I went to the grocery store and bought a fancy cut of beef, made a wine/mushroom sauce for it that was quite good. And that night, when we were watching television in our pajamas, you covered me with a blanket. We'd forgiven each other, and we lay comfortable in the groove of our life together.

We've become quite good at forgiving each other by now, have you noticed? Sometimes I want to say to people considering divorce from a marriage that's only vaguely bad, Oh, just wait. It just takes a lot of time, that's all. You'll see. Later, you'll be sitting together and you'll see the small lines starting in each other's faces, and though your hands may be in your laps they will also be reaching out to touch those lines with a tenderness you weren't sure was in you. You'll think, Oh well, all right. You'll have come to a certain kind of appreciation that moves beyond all the definitions of love you've ever had. It's like the way you have to be at least forty before a red pepper sliced in half can take your breath away. Do you know what I mean, Martin?

A certain richness happens only later in life, I guess it's a kind of mellowing. And now when I think of dying I think, Oh not now, not when I'm just starting to see. And I also think, don't let it be from something where I have to get my throat radiated. Don't let it be from something that makes me have a lot of pain. Don't let it be from something where I become a vegetable, or a burden in some other way. Let it be this way: Let me be eighty-eight. Let me have just returned from the hairdresser. Let me be sitting in a lawn chair beside my garden, a large-print book of poetry in my hands. Let me hear the whistle of a cardinal and look up to find him and feel a sudden flutter in my chest and then – nothing. And, as long as I'm asking, let me rise up over my own self, saying, "Oh. Ah."

Fifty years old. It is an impossible age in many ways. Not old. Not young. Not old, no. But oh, not young. What it is, is being in the sticky middle, setting one gigantic thing aside in order to make room for the next gigantic thing, and in between, feeling the rush of air down the unprotected back of the neck. I know that the transition is scary and full of awkwardness and pain – mental and physical. These dropping levels of hormones leave damage behind, like bad tenants on moving day who wreck the walls carrying things out. But once I get to the other side, I think I might be better than ever before. That's what I keep hearing. And when I think of it, that's what I've seen.

Have you ever sat by a group of older women out together at a restaurant, Martin, who are so obviously enjoying each other, who seem so oblivious to what used to weigh down so heavily on them? All of them wearing glasses to look at the menu, all ordering for themselves and then checking to see what the rest got. It is a formidable camaraderie I've seen among older women; I do look forward to that. I just wish I could cross over a little faster. I wish that this part of watching things go would not be so hard. Although maybe their leaving deserves to be mourned. Maybe mourning is the cleansing act that makes room for what follows.

I know exactly what you're thinking right now. And no, I am not cracking up.

The house I want will have much smaller rooms than the one we have now. I think we will have it built. There will be pastel walls, Martin, not the safe off-white you always insisted upon because that heavily jeweled, heavily perfumed, heavily made-up interior designer who came out when we bought our first house told us to let the things on the walls speak – not the walls themselves. *Neut*ralize, she said, looking at me because I had said I would like walls the color of the sun, and of robins' eggs. I don't know how we could have put so much stock in a woman whose clothes we both hated. The very notion of some stranger telling people how to arrange their houses seems so ridiculous to me, now. Did then, too, if you want to know. It's like someone else deciding when you're hungry.

I want a place by the ocean, where you can hear the water any time you decide to pay attention, where you can see it out of the windows. The ocean will be ever-changing during the day, blue to gray to green; but always the same at night: vast black. I want a white fence around the property, tall flowers leaning against it in patches so thick they don't suffer from the occasional thief. I want a porch, wide and long enough for an outside living room, perhaps a hammock for you, I think you might like to drink your seltzer in a hammock. You might like to read your Sunday newspaper there, too, then doze off under the business section.

Inside the house, a golden-colored wooden stairs should lead up past a small leaded glass window. The sunlight should come through that window so thickly it looks like candy. There should be no curtains in the house except for white ones in the bedroom, with trim so beautiful it's heartbreaking. I can find those curtains somewhere, I know – they'll be old, of course, and hopefully used, and therefore saturated with soul.

In the bathroom, I want an old-fashioned sink with a wide pedestal base; and the presence of a clear, strong blue color – perhaps in towels, and probably on the ceiling, too. There will be a claw-footed tub, and in the summer, I will paint its toenails, and in the winter I'll knit slippers for it. We'll have big seashells scattered here and there on the floor as though they had stopped by to change out of their swimsuits.

I want a small fieldstone fireplace, a bouquet of flowers always on the mantel. Multipaned windows, French doors. The kitchen should be a large friendly square and the cupboards should have glass doors to show this brown speckled bowl, perfect for making pancakes; that yellow mug, right for morning coffee. Our forks should be decorated on the ends with forget-me-nots so that each bite will carry flowers to our mouths. We can do without some of those damn wine-glasses, Martin. I would just as soon drink wine out of a jelly glass, it always looks so good in the movies when the Italian men wear their T-shirts and sit at the kitchen tables and drink their wine that way. And in the background, the women standing over pots with lively smells, wearing print housedresses and white aprons and braids pinned on top of their heads, and little, foreign, dangling earrings – I bet they have a nip too, their own glass on the counter beside them. Yes, I believe we must both start to drink from jelly glasses, and I think when we do, some stubborn old stone will be loosened.

The kitchen counters will be wooden, hip high, and a slight slope will develop in the middle from the weight of our meals. There will be a back door off the kitchen, a rope clothesline you can get to from there.

Our bedroom will have a little wall space for

paintings of flowers, but otherwise there will be windows. The bedspread will be white chenille. Our closet door will be large and heavy, and it will creak in familiar but different ways when we open it, as though it were saying the same word in different moods.

There will be another bedroom with yellow walls. For Ruthie and for guests. A round, floral scatter rug on the floor. Lace here and there. In summer, a blue vase on the dresser with one pink-and-white peony, the shameless-hussy variety. In winter, a fat book lying open there, pale sunlight on the page like a wash.

I want one bedroom painted a blue leaning toward purple, and I want that room kept empty except for the fill of light and the dust motes, drifting down like inside snow. It will be the place to stand in and get peaceful. To remember the fullness of spareness.

I want a little room only for me. Stuffed full of what I love. A ticking clock, too, the smooth measure of time that is not hysterical or guilty or full of longing, that offers no judgment of anything, that just says here, here, here, in slow, sounded seconds. Here. Here. Here. Off that room should be a small balcony, facing the water. Room for one chair and a begonia, a flustered red color. Room for one cup of coffee balanced on one knee.

There should be a shed in the back, with my red bicycle inside, a brown basket on the handlebars. Your bike will be in there too, though I know of course you won't want a basket, you think it's wimpy. I'll use the basket to hold loaves of bread from the bakery, packages I'm taking to the post office. We can ride to look at other parts of the ocean, to see the large and larger rocks, tan colored or gray, sharp or smooth. Waves will crash and the spray will be spectacular, as it always is, small cymbal sounds seeming to come from it.

We should keep gardening tools in the shed, and old newspapers stacked up neatly, just in case. You know. In case of paint. In case of puppies, in case of kittens, it's good to keep yourself open to the possibility of them.

You can do something in our new house just for you too, but this time *you* will ask *me* about it. It will be your turn to say, "What do you think about this idea, Nan?" And it will be my turn to say, "Well . . . I suppose."

Well, look how long this letter is, how I have gone on and on! This is so different from the usual way, when I try to cast my thoughts out, meaning to share all of them with you, and then slowly pull the line back in, your not having seen much at all. You stop listening so I seize up, or I seize up so you stop listening. Which is it, Martin?

I am in Minneapolis, staying at the Radisson, right downtown. Yesterday I bought cowgirl boots and a cowgirl hat. Black. Don't ask me how or why I found them here. They were in a store window and I answered the call. Then I had caramel corn for lunch and took a walk around a lake, there are lakes everywhere, here.

The boots were very comfortable, I don't think they'll hurt your picky feet.

Well, it was supposed to be a surprise, but as you can see now, I bought you boots too. And a hat. White, so you can be the hero. Which you sort of are, to me and to Ruthie. You know we both love you very much. I suppose in my own way I've been as neglectful as I accuse you of being. So let me tell you, to start, that I never felt scared of robbers when you were home. And I think your French toast is the best in the world.

I'm going to a movie now. Middle of the afternoon, in my cowgirl boots. Tomorrow I'm driving further north. I hear it's beautiful. And when I am there I am once again going to attempt sleeping outside. I don't know why it's so damn important to me.

Do not throw away any of my magazines. Believe me, I will know if you do.

Love,
Nan

Well, I suppose I did a very foolish thing today. On the way out of the city, I picked up a hitchhiker. He seemed so nice, that's the only way I can say it, standing there, his thumb out and his face a little embarrassed. Handsome thing. He got in and we got to talking and he told me he was coming from his girlfriend's house, well, not his girlfriend, just a friend who was a girl. I suspected that, this man was gay, I could see that. He said the woman was his best friend and they'd decided to have a baby together, that she was close to the end of pregnancy now and very testy, in fact she'd just thrown him out of her apartment and he'd had no way home, they'd been out in her car. He said he thought pregnant women were supposed to be easy to get along with, all dreamy and soft.

I said, Well.

He said she'd been cleaning like a crazy person and I said yes, the time is close, then, that was exactly what I'd done when I was close. Martin came home and I had been washing walls which I had never done in my life. He'd taken the bucket from me, saying, "Nan, Nan." It was kind of sweet. That night, at four in the morning, the contractions started. I'd awakened Martin and he'd said, "Well, you'd better try to rest a little more, you'll need your strength," and then he promptly went back to sleep. Snored! But I got up and went into Ruthie's room, which was all ready for her. I stacked and restacked her tiny T-shirts, wound her mobile, thought, soon I will know if you're a boy or a girl.

I told this young man, Ethan, his name was, I said, you know, a woman who is very pregnant needs a lot of very special attention. He said, well what could he do, he was there, wasn't he? He came to see her every day, he tried to do things for her, but she was just so damn cranky. And then he sighed and looked out the window and said he thought what she really wanted was for him to love her . . . that way. And he couldn't. I said that must be very hard. He said I didn't know the half of it. I said maybe he shouldn't go home, maybe he should go back to her apartment. He said yes he knew that, in fact he was just going to ask me to let him out and he was going to hitch back there, take her out to dinner, she liked the bacon burgers at the Embers, lately, although he himself thought it was not the best thing for the baby. I said I'd take him back to her house. He said really? I said sure. He asked me to stop at a florist's and he came out with two bouquets. He'd gotten one for me. Freesia. I said, Oh, but I'm on the road, they'll just die. So he went back in the store and bought a vase and he put the flowers in there and anchored it with a ribbon to the door handle. I thought, what a nice thing. And I was so happy I'd picked him up.

I used to always have interesting things happen when I picked up hitchhikers – not always pleasant, but always interesting. Once, a man had such terrible BO I had to leave the car windows open overnight. But other times I got to see the flash of a life like a peek at someone's true hand of cards, and I liked that.

On my twentieth birthday, I was out driving with a girlfriend and we picked up a man I have thought about a million times since. He sat in the back with his arm draped across the seat as though his invisible companion were along for the ride, too. My girlfriend and I were kidding around a little bit and he was laughing at everything we said and soon we were all laughing, it was the kind of thing where the laughter feeds on itself, where the sound of someone else's snorting and wheezing keeps you going until you don't even know why you started laughing in the first place – and you don't care. It's so good for you, that kind of hard laughter, so cleansing – you feel like your liver's been held up and hosed down, your heart relieved of a million grimy weights. We were driving down Lake Street, I remember, with the windows open and our elbows hanging out to an early spring day. The sun was high in the sky, "I Can See Clearly Now" was on the radio and I thought, nothing needs to be hard. I thought, I can suggest anything, and these two will say, "Sure!"

Before I had a car, I hitchhiked a lot, too. I had my fair share of nasty men pick me up; one said he "laid out stiffs" *for a living, and showed me his business card: THOMPSON MORTUARY, it said, in apologetic script. Then he asked if I would like to screw him, for a hundred dollars. He showed me the hundred-dollar bill, folded into quarters and stuffed into a corner of his wallet. I said, But don't you want to be in love, have sex with someone you really care about? I really said that. I think I thought I was a Mobile Therapist. He said no. I said, Well then why don't you just get a prostitute? He said, "I don't want a prostitute, I want a nice girl, like you." His voice was so oily and dark and it came to me that he could take me anywhere and do anything. When he came to a stop sign I said, This is fine, thank you, have a nice day, thank you, and I got out and went home and called my boyfriend Bob Sandler and he came over and got me to stop shaking. I wonder where Bob is now. I wonder if he still has his hair, he had beautiful hair.*

Another time I got picked up by a mother who was bringing her little son home from school, and she talked to him with great interest and respect about what he had done that day. I remember thinking, if I became a mother, let me be this kind. I was fascinated by the very notion of showing a child respect, it was outside my experience, my parents viewed children rather like puppies. The boy was about six, sitting with his book bag on his lap, idly fingering the clasp and having a conversation with his mommy and his insides felt right, I knew it. I thought, yes, let me be just like her.

I tried, but I don't think I succeeded. There is so much I'd do differently, if I could. Sometimes in the quiet of the afternoon, I sit in Ruthie's room thinking, an ache of regret lying like a stone in the bottom of my stomach. Not long ago I remembered how Ruthie always said, "Thank you, Mommy," whenever I bought her school clothes, and I burst into tears because she should not have felt she needed to thank me for what was her due. I shouldn't have said, "You're welcome." I should have said, "Oh, Ruthie, you don't have to thank me." Then I thought about how she also used to ask if it was all right to roll down the window of the car and I said out loud to her bedside lamp, "My God, I was so controlling. I'm so sorry." After I cried for awhile (and you know I'd been crying so often that week) I got up in the middle of this particular torrent of tears and made myself a bologna sandwich – anyway, after I finished crying, I called Ruthie and asked her if she thought I had done anything terrible when I was raising her. I said we were both old enough to talk about this now, and I was truly interested in knowing her real feelings. At first, she was kind of flustered, embarrassed – and she probably wondered if I were nuts – but then she said, "Well, mostly, you just taught me to trust myself." And I said did I really do that? and she said yes. And I thought how could I have taught you something I never learned for myself?

But maybe there was evidence for Ruthie's strength of spirit, all along. When she was in junior high school, that most dangerous of places for girls, she went through a very rough time with her friends. What happened is that she got pushed out of her group. I saw it coming, but I couldn't tell her. I had no idea how to say, Honey, I don't think they want you anymore. I thought they were crazy. I wanted to hurt them. I saw one of their group, Lindsay, in the drugstore one day when all this had started happening – the chicken calls, the way Ruthie's Saturdays were suddenly blank – and I thought about telling the clerk I'd seen that girl shoplifting – many, many times. I thought about grabbing her by her pert blonde ponytail and holding the spiral-bound notebook I was buying up to her neck. But I didn't. I smiled at her. I said how's your mother. I said tell her I said hello. And when, after a period of isolation, Ruthie determinedly brought home a new friend, I made cookies. The effort of starting a friendship was showing in both their faces, it was as though their underwear was excruciatingly tight. I overdid it, of course; I made three kinds of cookies, I folded the paper napkins into swans; I made a show of exiting so that they would know they were free to tell delicious secrets. They sat so straight and quietly at the kitchen table, and after I left I sat in the living room holding a magazine on my lap and craning my neck to listen to their soft, short sentences. I wanted to be able to tell Ruthie how to be popular, how to make and keep friends. But I was – and still am – pretty much a loner, one who wearies of almost anyone's company much too soon. My mother told me that when I was four, I came inside from where I'd been playing with another little girl, my first play date, and said she should go home now. Seven minutes had passed. Even when I got older, I'd be sitting with a bunch of college friends and suddenly have to leave. They were good-natured about it, they knew me. "Uh-oh!" they'd say. "Nan's gotta go, get out of the way!" I wanted Ruthie to be different from me, to be someone who could make casual conversation without clenching her fists, who could be comfortable at a party. Well, she is that. She is quite sociable. But she is like me, too. Thus the miracle of mothering. Thus the duck who puts her head under her wing but still watches her ducklings bustling about her, their heads held high.

Suddenly, I miss the scent of Martin. Isn't it funny, he has turned out to be the one I can be with the longest.

Dear Martin,

I am pulled over in a roadside rest. The sun is starting to go down, and the colors are spectacular. I thought that rather than risk an accident, I'd pull over and watch, and write to you.

I was thinking today that maybe you should retire, take an early retirement. Now, don't start huffing and puffing and thinking up all your fancy arguments. Just wait, I want to tell you something.

I don't regret the fact that I was the one to stop working to raise Ruthie. When we brought her home from the hospital I hovered over you every time you even held her. I knew you were her father and half responsible for her in every way, but I have to tell you, Martin, as far as I was concerned, she was really all mine. I made her baby food, I picked out her toys and her clothes, I took her to school every first day, I pulled her shades down for her naps, I took her to the doctor, I braided her hair and buckled her shoes and mounted her artwork on the refrigerator. And I wanted to. *I* wanted to. Once she got into the teen years, you and she seemed to get closer and that was fine with me, too. I had had my hands to her when she was still wet, was how I saw it. Now I could step back – keep watching, but step back. And then back further.

All during those years of Ruthie growing up, I was also the one to cook and shop and clean, and I didn't really mind that, either. Of course there were some bad days. Remember the time Ruthie was napping on a Saturday afternoon and I sat in the living room literally tearing my hair out and saying I was too *smart* to do this, that a chimpanzee could do what I was doing – better, that I had to have more challenge and stimulation in my life or I was going to die? I remember you trying to help, suggesting I get a job, and how I screamed at you that I could never do that, I couldn't leave her with someone else. It is such a violent love, that of a mother for a young child. And I had to be there, no matter the cost. I knew I was missing some things, I could feel some brightness of mind dulling; but on balance I loved what I did.

I remember once when Ruthie had just turned three. I was in the kitchen, I'd just finished putting everything in the pot for stew, and the carrots were such a deep orange, the peas such a deep green, and I'd gotten a beautiful loaf of peasant bread and it lay on the cutting board looking so . . . French. It was time now to just wait for the smell, my favorite part. I'd put in a few extra cloves, stuck them into a whole onion, in a line like a careless necklace. I took off my apron and came out into the hall and Ruthie had lined up all her dolls and stuffed animals along the wall and she was sitting before them on her little wooden step stool, holding a book in her lap. "What are you doing?" I asked her, and she said teaching school. I said oh, and I went into the living room and read the paper – well, I looked at ads for the fancy brassieres, read the recipes and the arts page – but mostly I was listening to Ruthie "read" her book about birds, one of her favorites. "Some birdies fly high in the sky," she said, in a high, clear voice that was learning pleasure. "Some birdies live in the nest." And then, ad-libbing, "with their mommies." I put down the paper and leaned back in the chair and thought, I can never be anywhere else. There is nothing that comes close to this. Outside, it snowed; fat, lazy flakes, drifting with soft intention toward the place they were meant to land.

I mean to tell you that I was mostly content, Martin. I carried on sometimes, I know, but I was mostly deeply content.

But now I want, well, I don't know, I guess I want a shared something with you. I want you to cook with me to do a marinade for the swordfish while I do the salad. What have you been working for, Martin, if you don't get the chance to do these things? I know you're not domestically inclined; I know you'll never take up needlepoint or quilting like some men do. But Martin, could you please just think about stopping work to see what happens? We are so lucky to have that option, why don't we use it? I don't want to go to Greece or Tuscany or do any of that fancy traveling stuff. I always hated traveling, you know that, the notion of figuring out how many pairs of underpants to bring used to make me depressed. You must be thinking that I've changed my mind, that I've begun to love travel, look at what I'm doing now. I know exactly how your face looks if you are thinking that, too, and the place in your cheek where your tongue is. But this doesn't feel like travel to me. It feels too much my own to be like travel, if you know what I mean.

So with our free time, if we get to have it, I wouldn't want to go anywhere. I just want to be able to sit down after supper and look at what's at the movies we can walk to. I want to take an afternoon to search out wildflowers – or, here, Martin, to look at fast cars. Wouldn't you like to do that? Instead of sitting at some meeting in an overly hot conference room, wouldn't you like to test-drive a Viper? We could do that, I'll wear a silk pantsuit and those three-carat earrings you gave me, they'll believe us.

I have a memory of my mother taking me outside in the rain. I don't think I could have been more than five. She'd been cleaning the windows with vinegar and newspaper, and I'd been sitting at her feet for the pleasure of the squeak and the smell. She had her cleaning kerchief on her head, a bright yellow triangle knotted at the base of her neck. It started to rain and she stood at the window watching, with me hiked up on her hip. She was quiet for a long time, but then she all of a sudden ran outside with me, whooping away. It was just pouring, but her face was directed right up to the sky, and she twirled me around and around and started singing some show tune really loud, I think it was an Ethel Merman song. I'd never heard her sing before. And then we came in and dried off and I never heard her sing again. Not once, not even under her breath, along with the radio. And the thing is, I believe she had a beautiful voice. I believe my memory is correct in this.

I am so often struck by what we do not do, all of us. And I am also, now, so acutely aware of the quick passage of time, the way that we come suddenly to our own, separate closures. It is as though a thing says, I told you. But you thought I was just kidding.

Martin, while I've been writing, the sky has changed from a pastel yellow pink to a dusky purple and now it's hard to see. But this dark is beautiful, too. It really is.

Love,

Nan

Today I woke up and felt the old pull of sadness back. It's like a robe that is too heavy, weighing down my shoulders, dragging up dirt as it follows along behind me. This was disappointing. I thought I'd escaped something.

I went to the window, looked out at a sky that seemed hopelessly vast. There were thick gray clouds overhead, swollen, pregnant-looking. I closed the drapes, went into the bathroom, washed my face, looked up into the mirror, saw the gray reappearing in my hair, and began to weep. Then I sat on the edge of the bed and gritted my teeth and thought, I am not going to do this anymore. I am so tired of collapsing into this state of grief, this achy regret about my thinning, graying hair, my wan-colored skin, my failing eyes and uterus, a year on top of a year on top of a year. A woman a bit older than me told me she recently found a hair under her chin and it terrified her so much she got in her car and drove for fifty miles — nowhere, just around in circles. It was a black hair, she said, stiff as a whisk broom. When she came home she locked the bathroom door and got out her eyebrow tweezers and pulled the thing out. She said she looked at it for a long time, and then she flushed it down

*the toilet – flushed it twice. After that she spent a good
fifteen minutes checking her face for more hairs. She said
she had heard about this happening, testosterone landing
on the female shore, but she thought it would surely not
happen to her. She was blonde, fair-skinned, had barely
ever needed to shave her legs. She said it was literally
horrifying, that her heart beat so hard when she found that
hair she thought for a moment about going to the ER, but
elected instead to drive around in circles, then come home
to tweezers and a locked door and a fervent prayer that this
was a one-time phenomenon, that it would never happen
again. It's so humiliating, she told me. It's like you're being
punished for something and you've no idea what you've
done wrong except age. She didn't really hear what she
said, she didn't hear the natural acceptance in her voice of
the idea that aging is a crime. But I did. And when I heard
it in her, I saw it in me.*

*But this morning I sat on the bed and I thought, I'm not
giving in to it. I'm just not. And I took out the yellow pages
and I looked for beauty parlors. I found one listed on the
same street as the motel I was in, and I checked out and
drove to it. It was a big, bare-looking place, highly polished
wooden floors, a hypermodern reception area, unrecog-
nizable music playing, hairdressers visible in the back with
the bored and slightly hostile faces of the fashion model.
The prices were outrageous. It looked, in short, like a good
place. I asked if anyone there could do a color. The
receptionist, wearing mostly her bones, but also a black*

blouse, a very short black skirt, black tights, black shoes, and deeply red lipstick, checked around and said Robert could do me in about twenty minutes. I said fine. She gave me a dove-gray robe to change into, very soft and smelling vaguely of some exotic perfume. Then I came out and sat next to a woman about my age who looked like she was in for color, too – she had the same incriminating line of gray beginning. She looked up and smiled at me, and I smiled back, then asked, "What are you having done?" "Highlights," she said. And I said that's the thing where you wear the tinfoil, right? and she said Yes, that's the one where you sit around looking like an alien reading a magazine. I said I'd thought about that, but it would mean a commitment to permanent color, instead of my temporary cover-up. She said, "I'll tell you what, I wish I'd never started this crap. I like gray hair. I always liked gray hair on other women. But when it happened to me, I ran right in here and got it colored."

They called me then, and a kind of pouty-mouthed young man draped me in silver plastic and said, "So what are we doing today?" I was going to offer my usual apologetic request – lately, when I go to the hairdresser, I always feel badly that I'm not a more exciting client, but all of a sudden I just got mad. (I also got a hot flash at the same time, which seemed sort of perfect to me.) I got mad for all the times I've had these snobby people work on me and not see me, stand over me yanking at my hair with their face turned away from me, chatting with another stylist. I said,

"Well I'm *not* doing anything. You, I hope, will figure out a way to get the gray back in my hair." I almost covered my mouth in amazement after I said this. I hadn't known I was going to say it, I really hadn't. But I realized at that moment that I did want my gray back, because in getting it, I'd be losing something else that I never really wanted in the first place: a corrosive sense of falseness, moving from the outside in. A sense of shame. Robert lifted up a strand of my hair as though it were dog shit. "Well, what's on here?" he asked. And I said whatever the last hairdresser had put on it. He said well that wasn't he. I said it certainly wasn't, that obviously coming to him once was quite enough for anyone. It had gotten very quiet in the shop. People had stopped working; the stylist at the end station had turned off his blow-dryer to listen better and his client sat still, looking out through hair that had been brushed forward over her face. And then a man came out from the back room, dressed in the standard black uniform. He had a way of walking that let me know he was the owner, or manager, or something. He kept his face turned slightly to the side; evidently no one was quite worthy of a full glance. "Is there some problem here?" he asked. And I said yes at the same time that Robert said no. The boss man raised his eyebrows, smiled a smile that looked as though it could be chipped off his face and used to open a can. "Well," he said. "Would it be something I can help with?" I said yes indeed. I said he could train his employees to be a little more human, to understand that when you came into a beauty *parlor you felt naked. And if you came into a beauty parlor when you were fifty you felt naked and invisible both, which was a very odd and terrible feeling they might want to be sensitive to, especially since older women tended to tip a lot better than younger women. From the reception room, I heard the sound of applause, the sound of one person clapping. It was the woman waiting for highlights, I was sure. The man asked, in a kind of tired way, what was it that I wanted, exactly I told him I wanted the gray back in my hair. He said well that was easy, all I had to do was let it grow. I said no, I wanted all the other junk that had begun fading to get off of there right now. He said they could try, but he couldn't guarantee anything. I said what else is new. He said pardon me? I said what else is new, you never guarantee anything, do you know how many times women go home from the beauty parlor and weep? He said he doubted that happened very often. The women with the hair combed over her face pushed it aside and said, "No, Henry, you're wrong. It happens all the time." Henry turned to her in a careful way. "Has that happened to you, Lucy?" he said. "You've never told me you've been unhappy with anything we've done here."*

The woman wanting highlights came into the room. Her cheeks were flushed a very nice pink, and her gaze was fastened on to Henry like headlights. "It's happened to me," she said. "Four or five times in the last year." "Well," Henry said, laughing a little, clenching his fists in a way that made me think it was so he wouldn't finger his collar.

"How can we know that if you don't tell us?" I said he didn't understand, that it was just a very intimidating thing to sit in a chair and have someone work on your hair. He said he didn't think it was so intimidating, it was just a matter of a client being open to change and new experiences. He said people make much too much of a haircut, it was no big deal, it was just hair – if you didn't like it, it would grow back. I said oh yeah well why didn't he just sit down and I'd work on his hair. He said you don't think I'd do that, do you? I said I know you wouldn't. And he told me to get up and I took off my drape and got my purse because I thought he was throwing me out, but what happened is he took my drape and put it on himself, then sat in my chair and told me, go ahead. I stood stock-still. I felt like my insides were taking the express elevator down. He turned toward the mirror, looked at himself, ran his fingers through the sides of his longish hair. "Really," he said, looking into the mirror at me, "go ahead." There was not one sound in that place, even the music had been turned off. Finally, I said, All right. Fine, I said. And I put down my purse and told Henry, "Over to the sink, please, I'm going to shampoo you first." He went to the sink and leaned back and I used the little sprayer to wet down his hair and I asked if the water temperature was right, which I thought was the least I could do. "Very comfortable," he said. I shampooed him and then I wrapped a towel around his head – rather inexpertly, as it turned out, it fell off as soon as he stood up. But he just picked it up and rubbed his head *for a minute, then settled the towel on his shoulders and went back to the station. I asked to see what was available for me to use. Robert opened his drawer. There were all kinds of scissors, five or six combs, a couple of brushes. I picked out a comb and a pair of scissors and Robert shook his head violently but Henry said, "No. Leave her alone."*

I combed Henry's hair for a while and then I held up a piece of it. I stood there for the longest time with the scissors open but then I just couldn't do it. I put the scissors down and said, Oh, just forget it. Never mind. He caught hold of my wrist, gently, and said, I want you to do it, go ahead, it's perfectly fine. I looked around the room and thought for a moment about whether or not I could get sued and how angry Martin would be when he called our lawyer, who did not have a good sense of humor. He was a good lawyer, though, fierce, he hardly ever lost a case. I picked up the scissors again, took a deep cut of Henry's hair. Then another. Then I said, "So how are things at home?" "Oy," he said, waving his hand. "Don't ask." And we both smiled.

I finished cutting his hair and it looked pretty terrible when I was done. It looked like a bad pixie cut. I said I'm sorry and he said, forget it, he kind of liked it, it certainly was different. Then he said, now it's your turn and I said you know, maybe I will just let it grow out and he said that would be the healthiest thing to do. He stood up and we shook hands and he gave me a sample bottle of clove-scented shampoo. The place was still absolutely quiet. I knew it wouldn't be after I left. I also knew that Henry had just done some terrific advertising for himself.

I got in the car and sat there for a while thinking. Then after I started driving I kept looking at my hair in the rearview mirror and it looked really terrible and I kind of wished I'd just kept my mouth shut and gotten my usual color done. But it seems some other part of me has taken hold, has grown huge and suddenly, like mushrooms after a rain. So my hair will look terrible for a while. Cost of admission to a better club, that's all.

Dear Martin,

I'm staying in a little place in northern Minnesota that is like a cabin/motel. There are six small, detached units: a little house for everyone, and everyone gets a tiny front porch, too. There's a kitchenette stocked with mismatched dishes and pots and pans, so I went to a grocery store to get some supplies. The notion of cooking again seemed appealing; you get tired of eating out. In addition to which I was eager to eat off the blue willow plate, there was one of those in the cupboard – a coffee cup with pansies, too.

When I got to the grocery store, the oddest thing happened. I found it very, very difficult to buy anything. I would pick something up, then think, no, it's Ruthie who really likes pineapple. No, Martin is the one who loves London broil. I wanted to get something special, a real treat, something I liked to cook and liked even more to eat, but everything I picked up, I put back. Finally, I leaned against the dairy case and thought, well, come on, Nan, what do YOU really, really like? And then I thought, my God. I don't know. I've forgotten.

Would this happen to you, Martin? If you went into the grocery store looking for something to make just for you (well, I know you never cook for yourself, but pretend you do), would you just walk right over and get everything? I think you would. I think you'd go right up to things, pick them up, pay for them, take them home, cook them and eat them with no sense of anything but pleasure. I guess you'd watch TV while you ate, or read the paper. There would be nothing tangled up inside you, no guilt and despair trying to work their way into the lettuce and baguette and breast of chicken. It is a case of feeling that you deserve things, that they are there for you; and it is something women seem to struggle with, almost without exception, and I don't know why. I don't know why men don't struggle with it. I don't know where your sense of entitlement comes from. Well, yes I do. It comes from the way you were raised, from everyone telling you, one way or another, that yours is the earth to inherit. That's true, Martin, and you know it, and there's no need here for any anger. I mean, I'm not angry, don't you be. I'm just wondering. I really am. I am just wondering and wondering and wondering. Goddamn it. All our lives, we hand it over.

Well, maybe I am a little angry. But it's not at you. It's more of a class action suit type thing.

Anyway, I stayed in that store for the longest time, walking up and down the aisles, thinking, Well *what?* I actually got pissed off at myself, you'll probably be happy to know. Finally I went over to the meat counter and bought the biggest turkey they had. And then I got all I needed for mashed potatoes and green-bean casserole and cranberry sauce and stuffing and pumpkin pie and my spirits started to lift. There was a radio in the cabin, and I was thinking, I'll find a good station, turn it on low, and I'll cook with utensils that are all new to me. And when the turkey is in the oven, I'll sit on the little sofa with my feet up and read *Family Circle* and *Woman's Day*. Maybe I'll make one of the crafts they show. I was feeling so happy about my plans, kind of excited.

But when I got home I found that the oven was too small to hold the turkey I'd bought, so I threw every-thing away and then I sat on the little bed with my hands in my lap feeling guilty and sorry for myself and then I went to a McDonald's and got a quarter pounder with cheese and the large-size fries and a vanilla shake and an apple pie and it tasted wonderful and it occurred to me that that's what I wanted in the first place, I was just too shy to tell myself, and so the universe had to sigh and shake its head and help me out, which it always will do provided we let it. This is something I have such a hard time remembering to believe.

While I ate, I chatted a little with a woman who was sitting across from me with three small, well-behaved children – a pleasure to see, in these times of over-compensating parents and children given reins so big to hold it makes them perpetually cranky. She was pregnant with a fourth, and she was wearing a faded blue maternity top with one of those silly bows at the neck. But on her it looked kind of good. She was a serene woman, very plain looking but also pretty, her hair held back with a brown barrette so simple and inexpensive and true it made me want to go home with her and be her child, too, I knew she'd do a good job bringing me up. There was an old couple there, out for dinner just like the commercial, remember that commercial I used to cry over where they go out for dinner at McDonald's?

I'm a little drunk now, Martin. I bought a bottle of wine and I see that I have finished a good two-thirds of it. It's rather an odd feeling, being drunk all alone. I don't believe I've ever done it. No, I haven't. I feel a little weird, which I don't like, but I also feel like I couldn't possibly be scared by anything right now, and I like that very much.

I just reread this letter and it seems I'm not making complete sense. However I will mail it anyway. You've certainly seen me worse. Haven't you.

Love,
Nan

Last night I read a magazine article about how girls get gypped in school. I am so happy this kind of thing is finally being recognized. They also talked about twelve being the age when things start to change for girls, the time when they start to lose their power, and I think they're right.

I remember coming home from seventh grade at the beginning of the year and having a certain routine. I'd get six Oreo cookies and a tall glass of milk. I'd go to my room and ask not to be disturbed, say I was doing my homework. I didn't do homework though, not right then. I'd lie on my bed eating the cookies dunked precisely to the pre-fall-apart stage and reading Hitchcock's Mystery Magazine. I allowed myself one story a day, and I made the last cookie and the story end together, and to this day I have never found a more pleasant ritual, including sex. After I finished reading, I would lie on the bed and think, I am going to be a writer. I am going to live in a fancy penthouse in Manhattan and have a martini served to me on a silver tray every night before dinner. I am going to have brown half-glasses and a big vocabulary.

After that I would look at my rock collection, which I kept in egg cartons at the back of my closet. And then I would think, I am going to be an archaeologist. I am going to wear my digging shorts on the plane. I am going to always be the one to say, "Here it is!" I will be covered with ancient dust, holding something so valuable in my hands it will make us all tremble. I will have a helmet stained with my own sweat and a leather backpack. I had such a clear vision of what that backpack would look like. There would be a place at the bottom for my teddy bear; no one would know but me.

After I did my homework, I would think, I am going to be everyone's favorite teacher. I will wear scarves and beautiful earrings so I will be fun to watch as I pace in my interesting classroom where there are no grades, where everyone passes so long as they try. I will say things so intriguing kids will say "Huh!" out loud. Every day after class a bunch of them will crowd in a circle around my desk until I have to say "Come on now, you'll be late for your next class," and they will all groan.

Then, at night, before I went to sleep, I'd read teen magazines, which I'd just discovered. I read about where hems should fall and how faces should look and what to say to boys to lure them and hold them. And I thought, wait. I don't think I can be this. It began to occur to me that I was a failure. I lost my grip. By the middle of the year, the phone replaced Hitchcock and my sure dreams of being everything. On my dresser, tubes of pink and coral lipstick *and sable-brown mascara appeared, blemish creams, concealer. Concealer, yes. The rocks in my closet got lost, and so did I.*

I remember some of that old flame coming back at one point, though. It was when Ruthie was a toddler, too young for school, too old to stay in the house for too long. I'd been making the most fantastic caramel rolls, improvising out of boredom until, if I do say so myself, they were extraordinary-tasting. I used to give them to the neighbors, Ruthie and I would deliver them in a basket with a blue-and-white cloth napkin, and they would all say the same thing, they would say, "My God, Nan, these are incredible." Most of the time their mouths would be full when they told me, they would be all excited. And I got this idea that I would set up a little stand at the T stop close to our house. I told Martin about it, I said I'd put up a card table and cover it with some homey embroidered tablecloth and sell the rolls for seventy-five cents each and it would pay for the ingredients and give me a bit of a profit and it would be fun for Ruthie and me and it would be nice for the commuters, to have something homemade to eat on the train. And when I got done telling Martin, he said, My God, Nan, you're serious? And when he said that, I saw all that I had said in another light, and I was so ashamed. I said Well, no, not really.

I don't know why I did that. I hate that I did that. I see little stands now at the T, places selling muffins and rolls and coffee and juice and everyone loves them and they turn a tidy profit and I happen to know they run out of caramel rolls first.

Something else. There was a period of time when Ruthie was older and off with her friends all the time on the weekends; she didn't want to do anything with her parents anymore. I would get up early on Saturday or Sunday and sit at the kitchen table and think, what should Martin and I do today? I would come up with this idea or that and then he would get up and say no to them all. Not overtly. He would say maybe and then not bring it up again until I did and then he would say God Nan you just keep harping on this stuff until I just don't want to do anything anymore! He'd get so angry and so would I and we wouldn't do anything. I would sit at the table again, hours later, looking out the window and think, those windows are dirty. I have to get them cleaned. And the phone would ring and neither of us would answer it. What was going on then? What was he angry about? Or was I the one who started everything? I honestly don't know.

Something else. I remember when Ruthie had gotten to her time of needing to hate me. I complained about it once at a girlfriend's house, and she said, "Oh, you know, the mothers always get it. They're home, they're in the line of fire." She told me about a day she and her sister were so awful that her mother sat down on the steps and stared at them through the railing, weeping and saying, "Oh please, you guys." We were very good for a while after that, my friend said. For about a week.

I thought of my friend's mother so many times after she told me that story. I saw her collapsing midstair, holding on to the poles of that railing to still her shaking hands and to beg her children to see her, to see her. I imagined her in her ironed housedress, her hair washed and held back with bobby pins crisscrossed neatly at the sides. She was trying, trying, trying, all the time, waiting at night for her husband to pass judgment on the roast beef, and that would be her grade for the day; enduring in the afternoons the spiky moods of her adolescent children. I remember my own mother serving dinner one night, dipping the big serving spoon into the casserole she'd made, and as usual one of us said we didn't like that and then another one complained and my mother dropped the spoon on the table and left the room. Very quietly. We all sat there, the whole family, stunned. And then in a few minutes she came back out, wiping her hands busily on her apron, her face splotchy, and she put the spoon back in the casserole and served it and we all ate it. And now I think, then what? Then, that night, she took off her skirt and hung it up on her skirt hanger and then she took off her sweater and folded it with tissue to prevent marks and then she washed her face, moisturized it, and went to bed in a blue negligee that my father bought her and later lifted out of the way while she stared at the ceiling thinking, I guess I am getting old, now.

Something else. About a week before I left, I was lying in bed, holding my rock, and I began weeping so loudly I woke Martin up. What is it, he asked, and I said my God

Martin I'm just so scared and so sad. He said why? What are you so sad about? I said I don't know, I just don't feel I understand anymore what life is for, what's it for, what is the point in it? He said there is no point. Then he sighed this big sigh and said, You know, Nan, ever since I've known you, you've looked for meaning and excitement in life. But life is by and large meaningless and dull. I said nothing, I stared at the still curtain hanging at the side of the window and in a few minutes he went back to sleep. I lay there for a good hour, not crying anymore, just thinking. And I see now that I was thinking he was wrong, although I didn't quite know that at the time. The thought was not in words, it was in the form of a dull nudge. And it was that nudge that got me to find this journal, and get going on this trip. And now, in my own stillness, I hear something. "Where have you been?" my inside body whispers to my outside one. Its sense of outrage is present, but dulled by the grief of abandonment. "I had ideas. There were things to do. Where did you go?"

What can I answer? Oh, I had some errands to run. I had a few things to do. I needed to get married and have a child and go underground for twenty-five years, be pleasantly suffocated. I meant to come back. But the bread crumbs got blown away.

Now I'm away. And leaving no bread crumbs behind me.

Well. Perhaps I will be a bit of an archaeologist after all.

Dear Martin,

  I went out to a mall today, and sat for a long time on
one of the benches. I had never done this, spent such a
long time watching the comings and goings of people,
and I enjoyed it. At one point, a young man sat next to
me, perhaps twenty years old, very attractive. He and I
struck up a conversation, he told me he had just
dropped out of college and his parents were furious at
him. I asked what he'd been studying, and he said that
was just it, he hadn't been studying anything, not really,
because he had no idea what he wanted to do. He was as
drawn to astronomy as he was to medieval history as he
was to Beat poetry. He even liked the business classes he
took. I said that was wonderful, that kind of wide
appreciation. He said he thought what it really meant
was that he just wasn't ready for college, what he was
ready for was living some real life. I said that sounded
reasonable to me, it wasn't like the days when you had
to worry about the draft. I said sometimes getting a job
and just waiting awhile was the best approach. He said
well, actually, he'd thought maybe he wouldn't work at

all, that he'd just . . . Ah, I said. And he looked at me and I was gratified to see that he was embarrassed. I asked him if he were living at home. He said yes, but it was no skin off his dad's nose, he was loaded. His mother, he said, was dead. I said I was sorry and he said, well, it was a long time ago. I said that even if his father were wealthy he still should get a job, that if he wanted to live real life, he needed to do that. He said he guessed so. Then he asked where I lived and I said outside of Boston and he said oh, was I visiting here and I said, well. And then I told him the whole story. He was fascinated. At one point, he even slapped his knee in approval. And then he sat back a bit and said, "So you were my age in the sixties, huh?" I suddenly felt very old and exposed, rather like my age spots had taken on a phosphorescent hue, but I said, yes I was. He said don't get me wrong now, but . . . free love. Was that real? I said, it certainly was. I wasn't embarrassed at all, which surprised me. I thought, if Ruthie asked me about this, I'd probably be uncomfortable. But talking to a stranger, well, that's different. What was it like? he wanted to know. I said well, sex just wasn't a big deal. If you met someone and you liked him, you were as likely to sleep with him as not. It was like a fancy handshake, didn't mean anything, really, didn't mean you were a couple. He said, I thought women liked commitment. I said some did, some didn't. He said, I thought all women did. I said, it was a different time. He looked at me rather closely then, and I could see he was trying to imagine how I looked back then, and I could tell when he saw it, too. His demeanor changed; he began flirting. He asked what was I doing for dinner, and I knew he was thinking, maybe I could get her. Maybe I could sleep with a sixties woman.

I remembered one morning not long ago when I got up and my hair was messy, but not unattractively. It was a day when I'd gotten enough sleep, and had not had too much salt or a drink the night before, and had slept on my back, so my face looked pretty damn good. Those days still happen every once in a while. I know you know that, Martin, you always say, "You look pretty, Nan," on those days and it is kind of a bittersweet thing because we both know that tomorrow I won't. But anyway, it was one of those days, I was having a good face day and my hair was correctly tousled and I thought I looked sexy, pleasantly whorish with my robe open too far, nothing underneath. I remember thinking, if I smoked, I'd have one right now, and I'd watch myself in the mirror. I reminded myself of women I'd seen in the movies standing around in their slips, their breasts full as melons and just hanging there, who would hold their streaked hair out of the way as they lit cigarettes at the stove. Well, I didn't smoke that day. I didn't even look at myself too long. Instead, I put on my waist-high white underpants and my blue bra and my gray sweatpants and T-shirt and I went to the grocery store.

I picked out the best plum tomatoes I could find and I felt wasted.

Sometimes I wish I'd had an affair or two, and sometimes I wish you had too, Martin. Is this a strange thing? Do you wish it, too? There is so much we don't talk about. Maybe you did have an affair. Did you? With that god-awful Jocelyn who used to work for you who was always making appointments to see you just before lunch or just before you were supposed to come home? I hope if you did have an affair it wasn't with her. Take the makeup off a woman like that and you have nothing but a pinched-nose whiner, you remember how she used to whine about her health problems, telling you she had a trivial scoliosis that made her back ache and that she once got "poison ivy of the blood"? Of course she also told you her underwear always matched, I was glad you told me she'd said that, but I was furious, too, because I knew for a fact that you found it arousing, that you probably had an erection start behind your desk when she relayed that very professional piece of information.

Anyway, it came to me that if I wanted to, I could have a little session with this young, young man and you would never have to know about it, he would be making love to history and so would I. But when I looked at him again, well, there he was with his gigantic knees and his unlaced sneakers and his carefully ripped jeans, his ice rattling around in his Coke cup – someone for a girl, not for me. I wished him good luck in whatever he did, and I left. I noticed he followed me for a while in a half-hearted, non-threatening sort of way, and please understand what I mean when I tell you that I hoped my butt looked good. I mean I just hoped my butt looked good, that's all.

Do you ever think about old lovers, Martin? Remember that party we both went to before we got together, the one where the tiny bathroom was painted black? I'd come to that party with one guy and ended up kissing another one in that bathroom. The guy I kissed – and ended up with that night – called himself some Indian name, Rishnu, something like that, anyway, he was dressed all in white and he had an incredible, calm, clear-eyed effect. He lay down with me later in the back of someone's station wagon and put his thumb to the middle of my forehead and told me to focus on it, to let the tension drain out through that place. I swear to God it worked. I was a little stoned; I thought that he had been granted all wisdom and sent to me for enlighten-ment, that he was an individual-sized serving of savior, and I was very grateful because in addition to being all wise, he was very, very handsome, and a terrific lay. Yes, he was a very handsome, blue-eyed man who used to dress in cowboy clothes and now dressed as a guru and it was fine, it all went together.

I just remembered that not long ago I saw your old dope pipe in the garage. Do you still smoke, Martin? Do you sneak a little now and then and not tell me? Do you think I'd yell at you? Maybe I would. But maybe I'd have a little with you. I wonder too, if you're still smoking dope, if that is where you put your soulfulness. Because you don't give it to me anymore, nor have you for a long time. I miss it.

You do know you can tell me anything, don't you? Have I made it seem as though you can't? If I have, I didn't mean to.

This is my last night in Minnesota. Tomorrow I'm moving on. Maybe the Black Hills. Maybe some small town where there are trees lining neighborhood sidewalks. But not home yet. You probably know that, though.

Love,
Nan

Early morning, the whole world seeming to be still and waiting. I am out on the porch with coffee and amazement. I spent the night with another man. How did this happen? It occurs to me that to start with seeing him come out of the woods would be wrong. It starts somewhere else.

There have been times, lately, when I have thought about suicide in a way so dispassionate I know it is serious. Oh, I thought about it in college, because everyone else was thinking about it, it was the artful thing to do. But I didn't mean it. It was a contagious fantasy, an imagined cure for many woes. Perhaps, rather than dealing with unrequited love or a forty-page term paper, we would kill ourselves. Every woman I knew had approximately the same vision for suicide, too; we would talk about it sometimes when we got together for pizza in someone's room late at night.

This was the scenario: we would have on eyeliner, no mascara. We would be wearing black clothes, one bangle bracelet. Our hair would be loose and flowing and extremely clean. We would be on our backs, barefoot, lying on a made bed, a poetic note of explanation in our pale, pale, hands. Dangling earrings would lie still in the small valleys behind our ear lobes, minute circles of color pooled uselessly beneath the gemstones. There would be a flurry of phone calls, people would weep and sigh and we would somehow be aware of this.

It was fun to imagine. When we were in classes we hated, we enjoyed it especially. I remember my biology professor droning on one day about invertebrates, and I closed my eyes and saw my own last breath – deep and satisfying, my young breasts rising up one last time to nothing. I was so captured by the image I jumped when a breeze came through the window and lifted my hair, reminding me of my own hereness.

But what I felt recently was not like that. Rather, it was like this: I would be coming home from the grocery store, stopped at a traffic light. I would look out the window at a tree, at a store-front, at a person walking past and think, oh, enough. There is nothing I want to see. There is nothing left. I want to be done. The car would be smelling of scallions and my front would be aching from my collar bones to my hips. It was a pain like hunger, but more hollow. And more acute. Then the light would change, and I would go home and put the scallions away and fold the paper bags up neatly and store them under the cabinet.

This happened frequently, this sudden drop into despair followed by the resigned resumption of my required life; and then, perhaps somewhere in the middle of making dinner, I'd notice that the pain had gone away. I would stand still to check; and yes, it had gone away.

One afternoon, I had taken a bath and I was standing in my towel and I dropped it and had a good long look and I did not recognize myself. I stepped close to the mirror, looked into my own eyes, and did not recognize myself. I put on a robe, walked around the house, from room to room. Martin's desk was dusty, and I used my robe sleeve to wipe it off. The phone rang when I was in the kitchen, and I stared at it, lifted the receiver and then hung it up. Then I turned off the answering machine so that when they called back I wouldn't have to hear who it was. They did call back, whoever it was, and the phone rang and rang and rang, which you rarely hear anymore, everyone has a machine that says, What? What do you want? Just tell the machine.

I went into Ruthie's room and I turned her bedside lamp on and off and then I stood for awhile looking at what was left there, what she hadn't taken with her to her apartment. In her closet were a few clothes, including the dress I bought her when we went to Mexico together. It had seemed so beautiful there, but I don't believe she ever wore it once we got home. Still, I was happy she'd kept it. On the closet shelf were some shoe boxes and I pulled one down, looked inside and found her Doggie, his ears worn thin as paper from her using them to rub her nose when she sucked her thumb. Once, when we were on vacation, she left Doggie at a restaurant. We drove back ninety miles to get him and I didn't say a word the whole way, I couldn't. Now he lay in a shoebox, treasured in absentia. I smelled him and I could smell Ruthie, the way she used to smell when she was little and had just woken up. I put him back on the shelf and I left the top of the box askew, so he could breathe.

I went back into the bathroom, intending to put on the clothes I'd brought in there with me, but I didn't. Instead, I sat on the edge of the tub and I was thinking, first I fill up the tub with water again, to help facilitate the bleeding. That much I know. There was an emery board lying next to the bathroom sink and I picked it up and drew a line across my wrists. Then I thought, no, that's the wrong way. You go up and down. To go crosswise is to be back in college, wanting the odd admiration that comes from wearing bandages over your wrists. This is different. This is coming from a true fatigue, a wish lacking in drama, flat with its plainness, but oh, so sincere.

I turned on the tap, and the tub started to fill. I got a razor from the medicine chest, the kind with one side protected, the kind you use to cut off calluses. I didn't want to hurt myself while I was hurting myself. When the tub was half full, I got in and put the razor to my wrist. I held it there, the sun glinted prettily off it, and I started to cut but then immediately stopped and got out of the tub and the next time the phone rang I answered it and I was very cheerful. I thought, most of my brain is normal. But somewhere in a dangerous corner, it is not. I thought, how long can I cross my legs and converse, put away the coffee cups, bring in the morning paper? I don't think much longer. I am so exhausted, I just don't think much longer.

So. That is what came before what happened last night.

I was sitting out on the porch of my tiny cabin, thinking, where do I go tomorrow? In what direction? I was imagining a compass drawn on a map, a smiling sun with four of his fat rays labeled in old-fashioned script, N,S,E,W, when I heard the sound of twigs snapping. I thought for a moment it was an animal, but then I saw the shape of a person coming toward me. I stood, backed up to the door, felt my heart beating in my throat. A man said, oh, sorry, did he startle me? I said no no, not at all. Yes I did, he said, and I said you're right. He stepped forward into the small island of yellow coming from my porch light. His hands were in his pockets, his face apologetic. He said he was from the cabin next door, he'd just arrived that night. I took a walk in the woods, he said. Didn't see anything. Didn't know how I could have, though, I didn't even have a flashlight. Got pretty spooked, he said, it's some intense dark out there. I said probably there was a flashlight in his kitchen drawer, there was one in mine. Right-hand side. In with the church key and can opener, all that stuff. He said oh really he hadn't looked in any of the drawers. I thought, isn't that the difference. The woman makes a home immediately; the man walks in to claim it, then leaves it. In my cabin, there was a glass full of wild-flowers on the little kitchen table. The towels in the bathroom hung evenly. My magazines lay neatly stacked on the small table by the sofa, a collection of rocks I'd found and admired nearby. Nan's here, the cabin said. If anyone wants to know.

I invited the man in for tea. He seemed so forlorn. He reminded me of little boys I'd seen standing on the edge of a group, so obviously excluded it broke your heart to watch them. He nodded, came through the door and I saw how tall he was, must have been a good 6′4″. I used to have a real thing for tall men — well, it was tall boys at the time. I wanted to be with a basketball player. I was tall myself, and it seemed very important to me to have the boy bend down far to kiss me. Nobody but a basketball player could do that. I only had one date with a very tall boy, and I was so excited I made a fool of myself. He never asked me out again. And he never kissed me, either, even though when he brought me home and we stood at my front door I laid my purse at my feet signaling my readiness. "See you," he said, and walked away. I watched him go, my tree man, my tower, my tall person who hated my guts.

After Ruthie was born, I developed a thing for beards. I asked Martin to grow one but he said no, he'd tried it once and it didn't work, there were bare spots all over his face where it just wouldn't come in. I said that was when you were younger, try again now and he said no. So I fell in love with our pediatrician, who had a wonderful beard. It was a play love, with a flame that went out whenever I was really around him.

So this tall man, Robert was his name, came in and sat in my tiny living room. Your cabin is nicer than mine, he said, looking around, and I said, oh, I'd just put a few touches in, that's all. I'd been there a few days, was leaving *tomorrow. He asked where I was from and I was suddenly very tired of explaining myself so I just said I was from Boston and I was on my way to visit my sister in Arizona, and I hoped he wouldn't ask any questions because I knew absolutely nothing about Arizona except that I thought you could get nice turquoise there. Of course I knew absolutely nothing about sisters, either, never having had one. But what brings you here, I asked, and he started to answer me and then, I couldn't believe it, he put his hands over his face and began to weep – racking, ragged sobs. I sat immobilized. I didn't know what to do. It is such a terrifying thing to see a man cry. I know it's supposed to be wonderful, men getting in touch with their feminine side and all that, but the truth is it makes me so uncomfortable I want to scream. Even when it's just men on the movie screens, I want to say, "Stop that!" I want to say, "Remember yourself, why don't you! You're a man!" It's a bad sentiment, it's wrong; but it's how I feel.*

Finally, he stopped crying and looked up at me, red-eyed. "I'm sorry," he said, sounding like he had a cold, which seemed suddenly like such a sweet thing, like a pale green shoot in an early summer garden, something you'd want to bend over and protect. I said no, no, it was fine, it was all right, was there anything I could do? He asked if I had some Kleenex and I went into the bedroom to get him some and when I did I had a thought: This is sexual, being in a bedroom, getting something to bring out to a man. He blew his nose – in the usual manly, honking way, I was happy to see – and then said, "I just . . . I'm sorry. My wife just died. I'm here to . . . I needed to get away."

"Oh, I'm so sorry," I said. He looked so young. I felt a million questions jostle for position in my brain. Died from what? Were you there? What did it feel like? What did you say to each other? And then Martin appeared in my head, alive, standing with his hands in his khaki pants, his blue shirt open at the throat. I had a thought to call him and say, "Don't! Don't do anything! I'll be right home!" And then the feeling passed, like a shiver does.

Robert said, "It was . . . well, the funeral was a week ago. Maybe it's too soon to be gone, but I just had to . . ." He stood up and apologized again, he was so embarrassed. I said listen, you don't have to apologize. He said it must be weird, seeing a man cry and I said oh no, not at all, hoping my face was not giving me away. He said well, looked to the door. It was very quiet. You could hear the low buzz of the living-room lamp. I said suddenly, I have a bottle of wine, would you like a drink? He nodded, sat down again, and I poured us two coffee cups full, and we began to talk.

He told me how his wife died, it was an aggressive form of lymphoma. from the time she was diagnosed until the day she died was only seven months. She was thirty-three. He said on the day they got the bad news, she came home and changed out of her dress and he saw her standing at the bedroom window in her slip, and he thought, this is the end of normal. I don't know how I'll live without her, he said, I don't know what I am without her. They had no children –

she'd not been able to conceive, and he said now he didn't know whether that was good or bad. I know children usually offer some compensation, he said, but if I had someone around with her face, with her eyes . . . Then he asked did I have any children. I said yes and I told him about Ruthie. I told him little stories about her growing up, from bringing her home from the hospital all the way up to moving her into her own place. He listened, but in an abstract way that let me know my words were just a calming distraction. He listened the way a child listens to soothing words from a parent; the content doesn't matter, it's the fact of a kind voice that counts, that works.

I realized at one point that my throat hurt a little from talking and I looked at my watch and it was 2:50. I started laughing and he looked at me and I said do you know what time it is? I showed him my watch and he said oh I'm so sorry and I said no, you didn't make me do this. I want to do this. My hair had started to fall down from the bun I'd put in so long ago, and I pulled the pins out and he said oh, you have long hair, that's nice. I said well, when you got to be my age it looked sort of silly, but I had always had long hair, I didn't feel myself without it. He said what do you mean "your age," how old are you? I had an awful temptation to say, How old do you think? but I hate it when people ask that. How they cock their heads when they ask that. Then I thought of saying, I'm sixty-four, so he would say how young I looked. But I didn't. I said, I'm fifty, and I felt ashamed. He nodded. The age of losses, I said, and he said, pardon? I nearly yelled. This is the age of losses! as though he were some wizened geezer sitting next to me cupping his hand around his ear. What are you losing? he asked. And what I thought I was losing in the face of what he had in fact lost seemed so ridiculous. My great tragedy is that I got to live past thirty-three.

I said, you know, it's so small. It's so egocentric. But I'm losing . . . well, my youth. My fertility. My sex appeal. I feel like I'm losing myself. It's so scary. I feel like all the self I've ever been is leaving, and this new self is standing at the station. I don't know who this new person is. Every day I look in the mirror expecting to see my old self back, and every day I have changed more into this new thing.

Well, he said, you haven't lost your sex appeal. You haven't lost your appeal at all, I hope this is all right to say. I sat still, said nothing. He said, you're a very attractive woman, physically. And you're attractive beyond that. You're very . . . present.

Well, I said. I couldn't look up.

He said, I remember when my mother went through her change. For a while, I think for a whole year, she acted crazy as hell. She was all depressed and weepy – used to lock herself in the bathroom and wouldn't come out, I don't know what she was doing in there, but it was bad, we had only one bathroom and six kids. But then, all of a sudden, she was done with that. She launched herself into a new life where she felt she could say the hell with anything she didn't like, and by God, she did say the hell with anything *she didn't like. She quit making dinner unless she wanted to, and she wanted to only about once a week. She wore these turquoise pedal pushers almost every day, big hoop earrings. She was really different, and at first this scared me, but then I realized I liked her better. She became a real person to me. She was interesting. After my father died, she moved into a small house that was entirely her. And she was happy, I swear, until the day she died. We knew exactly who we were burying.*

He stopped talking then, and I thought, he's remembering his wife, realizing she will never get older. He's thinking, what in the world is this woman complaining about. But when I looked up at him his face was full of compassion. Of kindness. And then he asked, wide-eyed and calm, if he could please brush my hair. I stood up, and I was a little dizzy – wine and fatigue – but I went and got my brush and sat on the floor before him and let him brush my hair. And I knew that I was his mother and his wife, and it was the most tender and full thing I think I have ever experienced. I closed my eyes, and I thought probably his were closed, too. When he was finished, he laid the brush down beside him and thanked me. I turned around, nodded. I said thank you. He said yes, all right. Then he stood, stretched, and I stood too, and he held me close to him, hugged me. And then, for reasons that now seem a little bizarre but then seemed right, he kissed me. And I let him. And then I took his hand and led him into the bedroom and lay down with him. We didn't kiss again, we didn't do anything but lie there, holding on to being alive and knowing there was nothing permanent about it. Morning came, we had some coffee, and then he left. We didn't say a word.

Dear Martin,

   We need to make a will. We need to talk about what
we want done at our funerals. We keep saying we're
going to do this, and we don't, but we have to. I don't
want to figure out what to do with our money, I'm sure
it will not surprise you to know that. But I do know how
I want my funeral, and I'm going to write it to you
because you never will listen to me when I try to talk to
you about it.

   I don't want to be buried. I want to be cremated and
scattered into the woods behind our house. I know you
don't like that idea, but I do. I want to be loose. I want
to have instant integration with the elements. Why lie in
a box delaying everything? And I am sick and tired of so
many cemeteries. There could be parks there, children
swinging. We can't fit all these dead people on the earth
anymore. I know you say you want to come and visit me
if I go first, that you want to have a spot to sit and
contemplate, but Martin, why get in the car and drive,
why not be standing at the sink rinsing out your coffee
cup and commune with me then? Why not sit in the den

in the afternoon and talk to me? I can be everywhere instead of in a box in the ground, some weirdly designed thing that costs a fortune. I can't be buried. What if I want to go somewhere?

Now the service. I do want a service. I am going to write something and I will update it if I need to, but I am going to write something for you to read to the people and it will have to do with trying to see the whole circle. It will be designed to let people feel joy, I would really like them to feel joy. Well, I would like them to feel pain too, to blow their noses into their damp hankies and shake their heads and say, jeez, that Nan; but mostly I want them to feel that this is a good thing, life and its hard, unexplainable ways, it is a good thing, and although I may have gone a little crazy at fifty, I loved my life. When everyone is on the way out, I want you to play James Brown's "I Feel Good." Really, really loudly. I don't care how old you are at the time or how you feel about James Brown, I want that song at my funeral. Every time I ever heard that song, I really did feel good. I always said, "Ow!" right with James a time or two, even though I was an uncool white woman who couldn't dance. I want picnic food after the funeral service, ribs and coleslaw and potato salad and brownies. At our house. And then kick them all out, Martin, even though there will be some who want to stay. Some will want to stay and say things to you, and some will want to stay because they are always the last to leave in case anything happens. Usually it's women, hovering around like huge flapping birds, but you just kick them out. And then you go in our bedroom and you pull down the shades and you take off your shoes and you lie down and you think of when we first met and you keep on thinking of everything you can remember about me up until the last day. Don't you dare clean up the kitchen and put away the leftovers before you do this. You just lie down and remember everything. That will be the real service. It would be kind of nice if you would talk to me, because we don't know, I might be able to hear you.

It's so funny, as I write this I think, but of course that won't really happen. Death. It won't really happen to me. This is just in case.

I've decided to stay here in Minnesota one more night. Then I'll be moving on. As always, I'll write from where I am.

It seems to me that your physical exam with Dr Singerman was scheduled for some time around now. Don't think you can cancel it just because I'm not there to make you go.

Love,
Nan

I am writing this by flashlight, which makes each word seem so important, so intentional. It is an odd feeling; a stage play by one to an audience of the same one.

I have built a bed in the woods, and it is very dark, no moon that I can find, no stars, only the very dim outline of the foliage nearest me, and then the rest of the world drops off. I can feel fear in me but it has stayed at the level of my throat: my head is clear and calm. The air is close, humid. There is the high whine of insects dive-bombing, full-time residents here who do not respect the rights of those who are not. Tomorrow I will have plenty of bites to scratch. Sometimes it is a pleasant thing; it feels good to scratch a bad itch, three bites in a neat row at the ankle can offer an odd sort of bliss.

There are the sounds of moving leaves, twigs snapping for this reason or that, a rare call from an owl or, even better, a loon. I have sat for some time trying only to be still. It is so much harder than it seems. I have always hated the notion of stillness, of meditation. It seemed, on the surface at least, colossally boring. Empty of anything I might be interested in. I tried meditation once. I bought a loose white outfit, I bought a book, I sat in a prescribed position; and my singular longing the whole time was for a watch I could sneak a look at. The book had said not to wear any jewelry, especially a watch, that time would become irrelevant. Not for me. After ten minutes, I was up looking at the clock on the dresser, thinking surely that my half hour was up. I was so resistant, nothing could enter my head: I saw no instructive images, I heard no wise words from a blurry source. No dramas played themselves out; no lighted center of peace was created inside me. All that happened in my head is that some huge foot began impatiently tapping away. Fingers drummed. My mind was straining at the leash, saying, oh, please, let me at least make a grocery list.

I put my meditation outfit in the bottom of my underwear drawer and I gave the book away. I thought, this meditation, it's a fad. A foreign import, like falafel. We are Westerners, and we cannot do this right, no matter what anyone says. Our speciality is rock-and-roll, cars, blue jeans. Ice cream. We are not inner-oriented. We are oriented toward sofas and television, convoluted politics, escalating sizes of popcorn at movies featuring escalating levels of violence.

Something just happened here.

I undressed, in the dark. I stepped out of my sleeping bag and took off my clothes to lie down on the earth. I lay on my back and I rested my hand on my belly, then moved it downward slowly until I came to the slight rise of my pubic bone and the tangle of rough hair there. I could see nothing, and so the feeling was more intense; and I felt more the toucher than the one being touched. I moved my fingers down farther, then pushed one inside myself, pushed up high until I found the tip of my uterus. I held my finger there for a long time, pushed across a message from me to me. Thanks. And forgiveness. Then I pulled my finger out and rubbed it along the inside of my thigh. It felt like blood, what I rubbed there. I was sure it was blood, it felt too thick to be anything else. I turned on my flashlight, excited, to look; but no, it was not blood, it was just dampness, colorless and not magical. Only of course magical. I could smell ocean. I tasted my own self's salt. And saw there was nothing to forgive myself for.

I lay down again, turned on to my front. I spread out my arms and my legs, and I thought, here. Here I am. I felt a pine needle dig into my thigh, and then I didn't feel it. I smelled the rich smell of black dirt; I felt something else's pulse in my chest; I understood with my belly that the sun was on the way within the next few minutes. I stood up and large hands moved into me and then separated themselves inside me, making me wider. I breathed in all I could take. And was, suddenly, myself again, overly aware of where the night space ended and I began. I sat down, waited for the pink of dawn to slit the bottom of the black horizon.

So.

So.

There is a feeling you have coming home at night when

you are tired, and the key turns so easily in the lock, and your sheets are fresh from your having changed them that morning. There is a feeling you have after your baby has nursed and now falls asleep on your shoulder. That is something like what I just felt. Only, the me-ness seemed to be removed, so that other things could enter in. It was a feeling of finding one's real place, I mean in the scheme of things. I felt as though I had, for once, the right perspective on death. It was a matter of the water drop seeing the falls, of losing the ego to the Wheel. But it was fleeting. I could feel my own longing for my own self return, my insistence on my own importance, at least to myself. It's funny; I always thought that to lose one's sense of self would be a horrible, disorienting thing. But it's not. It is a movement toward the deepest kind of relief I have ever known.

I feel as though this was a holy and personal event I will never share with anyone. That it cannot be shared, and should not be. Occasionally, one learns quiet, and then how to keep it. Even me, who has always felt that everything must be shared, in order for it to be.

Late morning. I am still here, outside, being inspected by squirrels and birds high up in the trees. I am sore and creaky, and a thin line of pain runs from my shoulder into the middle of my back. But I am exhilarated. I can roll up my bed and go back to the cabin for coffee and then I can drive to a new place. And then to another new place. I am only fifty.

Dear Martin,

Today, on the way out of town, I stopped at a Kmart. After I was done getting what I needed, I went to look at the gardening equipment. I always enjoy doing this; it's so hopeful, seeing all the spades and trowels hung up in shiny rows, all the big bags of lawn cures stacked neatly on the floor. Standing by the hoses were a man and a woman, a married couple somewhere in their early thirties, I'd say. They were discussing a coupon the woman held. Well, the woman was discussing it. The man was yelling about it. Apparently the woman wanted to go to another store to get the hose, because it would be cheaper there. The man was acting as though she'd suggested eating poison. "It'll take us fifteen minutes to get there!" he said. "Time is money, you know. Has that ever occurred to you?" The woman stood still, looking into his face, her own empty of expression. This kind of thing was not new to her. "I just thought . . ." she said. The man grabbed a hose, flung it into their shopping cart. Then he stormed off toward the checkout lane. I was happy to see that one of the wheels of his cart had been damaged, so the thing made a very loud, rhythmic, clacking noise that caused other shoppers to stare after him, smiling.

The woman stood there watching him go, the coupon at her side. And I thought, okay, Nan, this is the time you get to do something. Remember, Martin, when I called you from the airport and told you about the man who was yelling at the woman there? She was sitting in a plastic chair in an empty row, her head down, and he was pacing back and forth, just screaming at her, calling her a bitch, saying she was stupid, what the fuck was the matter with her? He went on and on and she never looked up. Her hair was long and blonde and parted in the middle, very fine, like baby hair. Her hands were in her lap. She wasn't crying. She wasn't doing anything. Everyone around was upset, you could see people start to do something, then walk away. I had a notion to go up and poke the guy with my umbrella, saying, "Leave her alone!" but he was so huge and muscular and angry – and clearly a little crazy. I looked helplessly at other people across the room, who were looking helplessly at me. And then I thought, Martin will know what to do. I called you and you said to get the hell away from them, it wasn't my business. You said not to speak to the guy, to remember I was in New York, the man would probably shoot me if I asked for the time.

After that I hung up, I put my umbrella under my

arm and started toward that couple. I wasn't going to mind my own business. When I got close to them, though, I saw that a security guard was coming toward them, too. I thought, oh good. The security guard talked in low tones to the man and the man nodded as though he were ashamed. Then, as soon as the guard was out of sight, he started in on the woman again, and although he had lowered his voice, his fury had clearly escalated. I thought, later, she'll really get it, because someone told the security guard to go over there. It will be her fault, just like everything else is her fault: a button that falls off his shirt, slow service at a café, the level of humidity. The woman's legs were crossed, and as still as the rest of her. Her ankles were long and slender, thoroughbred-looking, and there was a tattoo around one of them, like a bracelet. It looked like roses and thorns. And I remember thinking, first, we'll get rid of that tattoo. But then my flight was announced and I walked away. And I have always regretted it.

So when I saw this incident at the Kmart, I thought, not this time. I'm not walking away this time. For one thing, the husband was short, a half-bald guy, nerdy-looking in his checked pants and knit shirt. I figured, if need be, I could probably punch him out.

I nodded to the woman and she, embarrassed, nodded back. And then I said, "Would you like a ride home?" She looked at her husband, standing in line and glaring across the room at her. Then she looked back at me. "Yes," she said. "Thank you. But not home, if you don't mind." I said, "No problem. I'll take you anywhere you want to go." I put down my shopping basket; I'd get deodorant and gum and toothpaste somewhere else. When we walked past her husband, he said quietly, "Hey. What are you doing?" And then, loudly, as we continued walking toward the door, "Hey! What are you *doing*?" The cashier said, "Sir? Are you buying this?" And the guy pushed his cart up and got his wallet out. I led the woman to my car.

I started driving and she started talking. Her name was Lynn; she'd been married for five years; the kind of treatment I'd witnessed was not unusual. I asked if he hit her and she said oh no, never. She said that might be better actually, then she could watch something heal.

I took her to a Wendy's. We had a Coke and talked a little and she seemed to feel better – when she smiled, I saw that her teeth crossed endearingly in the front. She asked if I would mind if she got herself a burger as long as we were there, she loved Wendy's hamburgers. I said no problem, I was in no hurry. I said I had a fondness for singles with cheese myself, I'd join her. When we came back to the table again, she asked if I had just moved here – she'd seen my out-of-state plates. I said no, I was just passing through. And then I said, "How come you married him?"

There was a long moment. She stirred her Coke

with her straw, then said, "You really want to know?" I said yes. She said it was a rebound situation, that she had been dumped by someone she really loved and it hurt so bad she just wanted to marry someone else quickly and be done with it. She said she had tried so hard to get her old lover back but the last time they were together, she'd made a fool of herself, flung her head into his lap and wept and felt only the slight movement of him trying to pull away. She said, "I thought, anything is better than this." Her husband had always had a crush on her, he'd lived on the same block when they were growing up and he was always trying to get her to go out with him. So she called him and they went out a few times and then he proposed and she said yes. "I felt numb," she said. "I felt like I was watching someone else do this. The last week or so before we got married I would wake up very night crying. I knew it was wrong. But I did it anyway."

I asked if she had children. She said no. And then she said, I know what you're going to say. But I can't leave him. Every time I try, I just end up coming back. I don't see that there's anything that special out there. Everywhere I look it seems to me that even the women who are supposedly happy, they're just pretending. I said oh no, you're wrong. She looked at my wedding ring, asked me, are you happy? I said well yes, that we had our problems, but I would say I was happy, I was glad I'd married my husband and I'd do it again. (I would, Martin, only I would not wear that dumb dress, I would wear a nice white two-piece suit.) Lynn said, so you never get that thing, where you're saying, here is the wife, making dinner for the husband. I said what do you mean. She said oh, you know, that thing where you feel outside yourself, you're watching yourself, and you're not sure at all where you *really* are. I said, well. I said I guess I feel that sometimes. And I realized that of course I do. Then I watch my hands peel the carrot and realize I am not quite there. And oftentimes, then, I look up out of the kitchen window and there is a dull pain in me. I never know what the hell it is, really. I look out the window, watching for birds, and wait for the ache to pass, and it does.

I don't mean to say this is your fault, this pain that comes, because it's not, Martin. I do mean to say that this trip has made me aware of so much I'd kept hidden from myself. And now that these things are out, there's no putting them back, they're like those sponge things that grow forty times their size.

I guess this sounds like a warning. And perhaps it is. But I want you to know that I want to live with you, I don't want to be without you, it's not that. You're the only one whose driving I trust enough to go to sleep in a car. Every time I ride with someone else, I feel I have to watch the road, too. Blinker, I'm thinking. Brake, brake! It's kind of exhausting.

Oh, Martin, and you're the one I want to watch

television with, I don't mind folding your socks, we can fart in front of each other, that means more than a new bride thinks. And you're the one I always want to show things to. I always need to show you. Remember the last time I went to the grocery store and I called you into the kitchen to show you the smoked turkey I'd bought? Oh, you said. Uh-huh. That was gentle of you. I realized after I'd done it that you could have said, *Nan*.

I had a thought the other day, what if Martin is keeping a journal too? I got so excited by the idea. I saw your neat handwriting in a brown leather journal, a handsome, manly thing. I thought, boy, would I love to read that. I like it when I get a peek at your insides. Of course whenever I tell you that, you close up like the takeout window at that ice-cream stand we go to every summer. I always think of that, when I ask you to reveal yourself more, that you are like the man wearing that little white paper hat, sticking his face out the window to ask what you want and then slamming it shut when he hears your request. I have to come at you in more indirect ways. I remember once we made these lists that were a suggestion from some woman's magazine. I'd bought the magazine so I could make the roast pork tenderloin shown on the cover. But there was an article I found in it, things to do to bring couples closer. We were to write the five things we prized about each other, and then the five things we'd like to change. You were in a rare, cooperative mood that night, and you agreed to do it with me. We got shy about telling each other what we prized and then we got in a fight over what we'd like to change, remember? We went to opposite ends of the house and then, an hour or so later, you came up into the bedroom where I was reading and said, "I'm going out." I said I could not care less. You said, "I'm going to Gallagher's." I said, for a steak? Yes, you said. Well, wait, I said, I'm coming.

Martin. We have a lot. Some people have so little. I took that woman home and I watched her pick a few weeds out of the cracks in the sidewalk on her way up to her door. She said her husband would probably be too scared to be mad anymore. He always thought she was going to walk out on him. I said, well, you'd think he'd change how he treats you then. And she shrugged. There were no tears in her eyes. There was no frustration. There was only a flatness, which I found so frightening.

It's six-thirty. I'm in a little town in South Dakota. There's a great-looking movie theater here, the Grandview, it's called, all old-fashioned looking, an old lady with cat-eye glasses selling tickets, a blue cardigan sweater hanging on to her skinny shoulders. There's an ice-cream shop next door, stools lined up at the counter, menu on the wall in a curly black script, and I saw they have patty melts. My night is cut out for me.

Tomorrow I'm driving exactly one hundred miles

west. Then I'm turning around. Please make an appointment with that builder we like, Peter Quigley. Make it for a few weeks from now. Please.

Love,
Nan

Eight-thirty p.m. I'm staying at a turquoise-blue motel, a neon sign in front that's a pink flamingo, his wing waving you in. How could I resist such a place? There's a bathtub-sized pool, a family of four enjoying it as though it were Olympic-sized, as though it belonged to Esther Williams herself. The mother, her hair piled on top of her head, sits on the edge of the pool and occasionally dips her baby girl, maybe eighteen months old, into the water, then out again. I can hear that baby's squeals even through my closed windows, and I smile every time. Her diaper drips happily; her legs kick the air. The father is playing ball in the water with his son, an exuberant blond boy maybe four years old, whose bright-orange trunks hang on to hips that look like little folded wings. When he gets out of the pool to retrieve the ball, his knees knock from the cold; he wraps his sticklike arms uselessly around himself, and his teeth chatter. Close up, I know, you would see that his lips have turned a bruised color, requesting warmth. Twice now I've heard his mother say, Timmy? Aren't you too cold, honey? Don't you want to go in, now? And twice I've heard him say no!

A swimming pool in the summer pulls children like a magnet. They are helpless against it. The water is silk on their skin. They appreciate everything: the drops of a splash that refract into rainbows before them; the muscley pull of their own arms carrying them across the wide surface (shipwrecked! their brains scream); the sudden quiet and undulating view when they submerge themselves, the Walt Disney quality of their underwater voices. When you become a grown-up you mostly stay out of the water, sitting in an itchy plastic chair and reading a magazine, mildly irritated. You don't go in unless you're so hot you're faint or you are playing with a child and therefore on duty. You have learned that the water is not jewel-like, see-through blue; it is only that the sides of the pool are painted.

I've been staring at the phone, wondering if I should call Martin. This is the strongest the urge has been. But every time I reach for the receiver, something stops me. I guess it's just not time. I guess I want to be completely finished before I start talking to him, so I'll know the right end of my own story.

I stopped at a farmhouse today. I'd been on a country road, passing lush field after field of this or that. Once, I came to a field full of daisies, a beautiful white house set back from it, and there was a sports car with Texas license plates parked in the middle of the field. A young black man was sitting in the car, waving at another man who was taking his picture. The man in the car was smiling widely, so happy. I thought, later, he will look at that picture and

*think, God, that was a good day. Where was that field? I
had a notion to stop and talk to them, to say what are you
doing? Where are you going? What kind of car is that? But
I didn't, I kept on as though I had an appointment, and
perhaps I did. Because at the next farmhouse I came to,
there was a woman sitting out on a rocker on her front
porch, a big white enamel bowl in her lap, a paper bag of
something at her side. I thought, oh what if those are peas
she's shelling? What if she'd let me sit there with her? I
turned down her driveway, a cloud of dust rising
magnificently after me.*

*I stepped out of the car, and she nodded at me, smiling.
"You from the phone company?" she asked, shading her
eyes from the sun. I said no. "Oh," she said, and took her
hand down. "Well, I got a busted phone." Then she looked
expectantly at me, waiting for me to explain myself.*

*"I'm just . . . I was passing through," I said. "I saw that
you . . . well, it looked like you were maybe shelling peas."*

*The woman looked into her bowl, then back up at me.
She said, "I am. I don't sell them. I'll give you some,
though." I said oh no, thank you, that wasn't it, it was just
that I'd always loved the notion of sitting on a porch on a
farm, listening to the sound of peas falling . . . you know . . .
into a bowl . . .*

*She was looking at me a little funny. Not like she
thought I was crazy. Just short of that. I took in a breath,
shrugged. I said, Well, would you mind if I just sat here a
bit? She said, I don't know, I guess that'd be all right. She*

asked if I'd like a chair and I said no, the steps were fine. Drink? she asked, and I said no, really, I was fine.

She was quiet for a minute, then asked slyly, So are you one of them moviemakers or something? I said oh no, I was just an ordinary woman, out on a trip, Nan was my name. Eugenie, she said, pleased to meet you, and I heard the sound of peas kerplunking and I smiled. What, she said, smiling herself, and I said, oh that sound, I just loved that sound especially when someone else was doing it. She said she guessed she was used to it, she herself preferred the radio, only that was busted, too. I asked her what kind of music she liked, and she said any kind that would come in. Although she was partial to that Tony Bennett fella. She liked fancy music, too, them violins. Right, I said, me too. She said, "Course, when you're shelling with someone, why then you talk, and that's better than the music." She said there used to be a lot of women living around her who would get together on summer afternoons, shell peas for the dinners they would be making later – shell the peas, clean the corn, slice the tomatoes, peel the potatoes. "We'd all set out here," she said, "getting a start on things. We'd talk so hard sometimes." She looked away from me, out over the land in front of her. "They is every one of them gone, now," she said. "Dead, or moved into one of them nursing homes." I'm sorry, I said, and she said, "Well what are you going to do, got to get old and move along, make room for the next wave. I just always wondered who'd be the last one gets to stay in their own home. Turned out to be me. Huh! Sure did."

I asked her old she was and she said eighty-six on her next birthday, which was in a month. I guess I looked surprised because she said I know, I know, I don't look eighty-six, everybody tells me that. We got good skin in the family, goes a long way back. Swedish.

Her phone rang then, and her head jerked up, eyes wide. Then, slowly, she went into the house to answer it. When she came back out, she said, "Danged if it ain't fixed. And they never did even come here! Fixed it out . . . there, somewhere." She shook her head. "I sure don't understand how things work no more." She rocked a bit, then said, "I 'spose you got one of them home computers." I said yes, we did. What for? she asked. I said well, my husband used it for his work, and he did our finances on there, I used it to write letters . . . Write letters? she said. I said yes. She said, you mean you don't write them on stationery? I said no. She said well pardon me for saying so, but that's a crying shame. What with the stationery they got now. She said, I was in town the other day at the Hallmark, and the stationery they had there, it took my breath away. Birds and seashells and flowers and cut-lace edges, some designs so beautiful I felt the tears start. You know how they do, she said, when you like something so bad. I said yes. Well, she said, tell me true, wouldn't you rather get a letter on that kind of paper? I said I guessed she was right. I didn't want to get into the fact that it was a rare person who wrote a letter at all anymore.

I said, so what's it like, being eighty-six?

She laughed, then rocked for a minute, thinking. I watched her feet, she was wearing blue Keds and the thin white socks that little girls wear. Finally, she said, well, it's painful, your joints hollering about something all the time, this thing kicking up, or that. She said, "Seems sometime like you get one thing locked out the front door, the other one sneaks in the back. But it's not as bad as some folks make it out to be, folks like to exaggerate, makes them feel important. They got to make everything a red-flag emergency. You take this change of life thing, why, you can't hardly pick up a ladies' magazine and not see some big story about it, when it's just as natural as a sneeze."

I said, well. I said, it probably depended on the person. Well of course, she said, everything depended on the person, but the meat of the thing was this: you accept change in your life or you might as well be dead.

I looked down, and I said perhaps it was difficult for some people to accept certain changes, that it took some getting used to. She stopped working and leaned toward me. I could smell peppermint on her breath. She said, "Oh. I see. You're having a hard time with it, is that it?" I said I thought I was, but that I might be getting better now, that this trip had helped me. She said well, that's good. Then she sat back and said, you know, I'll tell you the truth. It hurt me at first, too. But then it was over, and I saw I'd just been scared of it, that's all, big black thing coming down the road at me all dressed up like death hisself. But then! Why, I come to see it was just a little pocket in my life, a small place, really. I remember telling my friend Katherine about it, she was a few years older than me, she was out hanging the sheets and I was sitting on her back steps. I remember thinking it was the last day she'd get to do this for a while, the weather was turning. Anyway, I said, Katherine? I think I'm over all that blue way of thinking. And Katherine, she had her clothespins stuck in her mouth and she took them out and looked at me and said, well now, what did I tell you? You were running around waiting for something so terrible to happen. Like a big wing was going to grow out your forehead, you'd be some kind of freak, when the truth is, happens to every one of us. Think of the poor men, she said, they got to go bald. And then they can't even do it no more and that's about 99 percent of their lives!

Eugenie said Katherine had chickens on her farm, and there were feathers on the ground here and there. What could I do, she said, but stick one of them feathers on my forehead and then call Katherine? Yoo hoo, I said. Does it look very bad? We 'bout busted a gut, she said. Relief, that's all, the two of us saying I'm right here with you, don't be scared. That's one thing about people, Nan, you always got a lot of folks right with you.

Then she asked if I were one of them authors. I said no. I said I kept a journal, that's all. She said, well, come in the house anyway, I'd like to show you something.

I followed her in, and she handed me a thin stack of papers, folded into thirds and tied with a wide blue ribbon. These are poems my husband wrote me, she said – she pronounced it "pomes." I'd like you to read them. I'll make us some blackberry tea.

I sat at the kitchen table and read his poems and I had a thought to ask her if I could copy them, but I didn't. They were beautiful things, I remember one was about him looking at the flowers in their garden. He wrote something like, what were we, that we got to witness such a thing. He said that when he saw the shade of burgundy on one petal progress to a pale shade of pink, he couldn't do anything but stand there with his hands at his sides, and that the emptiness of his hands felt heavy. And that that was how he felt about Eugenie, he would be coming in from the fields at night and see the light on in the kitchen and his hands would feel heavy again.

I wish I had copied them. I would like to read them again now. Anyway, I told Eugenie I thought they were wonderful. She sat down at the table with me, nodded, said, yes, I think he was a regular Shakespeare type. But you know, he never did show me them poems. I found them buried in his bottom dresser drawer. I think he thought they weren't good enough. She took off her glasses, rubbed her eyes. Her lids looked like tissue paper, but the blue of her iris was still strong and clear. He was a good man, she said. I never did hear him complain. He never was the kind to worry about cold mashed potatoes, he would just eat them. You know.

I left soon afterward. I drove about a mile down the road and then pulled over and wept. I was thinking about

Eugenie coming across those poems after her husband's death, then sitting back on her heels to stare into space for a long time.

Dear Martin,

First, when I come home, I'm taking a nap. Then I'm taking a bath. Please make sure there's some of that Damask Rose in the linen closet, that's the one we both like best. Then I'm putting on that red dress you like, the one that pushes my boobs up to my chin. And my red heels. My black nylons. Like you like.

We're going for dinner to the Capital Grill on Newbury Street and if we have to wait three hours to get seated, we'll wait three hours. We'll get drinks and talk, I have a lot to tell you.

I'm getting everything to eat, and I think you should, too. Appetizer. Dessert. After-dinner drinks. I like being in that restaurant, despite its nearly palpable male ambience – dark oak walls, dim lights, a wide sense of red; even oil paintings of hunting dogs with dead birds hanging from their mouths, for God's sake. It's the place I've always felt the friendliest toward males – admired them, envied them their easy comfort and their generosity, their tendency to tip big and eat the same way. I've seen groups of men out to dinner there, sitting at a round table and, in the absence of their wives, cheating – with porterhouse, with fried onion rings, with cheesecake studded by chocolate chips. They talk loudly and laugh louder, move back in time to summer nights when they would meet at the all-night diner after they'd taken the girls home, to talk about what they got, to talk about cars, to talk about who was going where tomorrow. I got to do that once, hang out with the boys after their dates. I was visiting my aunt and uncle for two weeks one summer, and one of their sons was my age, sixteen. His job was to entertain me, and his notion of how to do that was to wordlessly bring me along with him everywhere he went. It was fine with me. It felt like rare privilege.

So I got to go to the all-night diner, and my cousin explained over his massive-sized cheeseburger that if someone came in with his shirt untucked, it was to cover the stain of him coming in his pants. I got to lie on the floor of my aunt and uncle's bedroom, using their extension to quietly listen in on my cousin's phone conversations as he paced in the kitchen below me; and I observed with a wrinkled-brow wonder how comfortable boys were with long silences on the line. I got to stay up late with him, watching black-and-white movies featuring angry gorillas, while he carped at his younger sister and brother to buzz off, to get the hell to bed. Once, alone, we tried kissing, but we frightened ourselves out of that in a hurry. We were envisioning offspring with three heads. Worse than that, we were envisioning confessing to our priests that we'd French-kissed our cousin, and gotten damp in the pants to boot.

I got to sit with the boys on the beach and hear what they said about every girl's body that passed by and I have to say I usually agreed with them. I got to set off cherry bombs in rich people's neighborhoods, although my slow running once nearly got all of us caught. I was called by my last name, just like one of the boys. And then one night when we were out cruising, I started making out in the backseat with Whitey O'Conner, and everything got ruined. I ended up staying home with my cousin's younger sister after that, playing with her pet rabbit and wishing I'd kept my femaleness tucked in.

I don't know if I ever told you this, Martin, but whenever we go to the Capital, I always want to be a man for a little while. I want to feel back in that circle. I want to be wearing a suit with a vest with the bottom buttons undone due to the deliciousness of my dinner. I want to be slouching back in my burgundy leather chair, my mouth making those fish movements in order to smoke my fat cigar, nobody around me complaining. My wallet would be thick with large bills. Men always carry more money than women, did you ever notice that, Martin? All other things being equal, a woman will have maybe forty-five dollars, a man will have a good hundred and fifty.

After the restaurant, I want to walk down Newbury

Street, which you never want to do, you always just want to go home and walk around the house in your underwear and then watch the news. But this time I want to walk down Newbury Street in my heels with my hair up, holding hands with you and pointing to the artwork in the gallery windows, to the outlandishly expensive wedding dresses, to the books so attractively displayed in the windows at Waterstone's you have to ball your fists to keep from smashing the glass and stealing them. Just be ready, Martin, we are not going home right after we eat. We might go to the North End, drink cappuccino at the Paradise and hope some gangsters come in to use the pay phone.

I'll pay for dinner at the Capital. I'll sign the receipt with a drunken exuberance that makes my penmanship curly. When we get home, I'll screw your brains out. Like we used to. You can leave the lights on now. I don't mind anymore. I think I understand the purpose of my body. And then you can walk about in your underwear and I'll walk around in my robe, Kleenex in the pocket in case I want to blow my nose to Ted Koppel. Our voices will be low and sleepy; only a few lights in the house will be on. The recliners built into our family room sofa will seem less a joke and more a necessity: we will be ourselves and loosely comfortable.

Also: some Sunday we are going to rent a canoe and paddle down the Charles. We are going to music festivals when we see them in the paper, and we are going to Harvard Square to throw money into the upturned derbies of the jugglers. Think of how many weekends we've spent going to the cleaners and to Lechmere's, to look at things we already have. I am so tired of that. It's so unnecessary.

Martin, I want you to do something for me. In the family room, there's that picture of me when I was twenty. In front of it you'll find a silk flower. I don't know if you ever noticed it before. I think I put it there because I was grieving for the loss of that self, it was like an altar offering to the person I used to be. Get rid of it, will you? Throw that flower in the garbage, where it belongs.

Love,
Nan

P.S. For the screw-your-brains-out portion of the evening, Martin, I wouldn't mind your buying me a little something to wear. You know what I mean.

Last night, I was thinking about my grandmother. I was remembering a time when I was eleven years old, and lying under her kitchen table in my new pink pedal pushers and matching pink-and-white-checked blouse, my ankle crossed over my knee. I was listening to my grandmother and her five daughters – one of them my mother – talking. I loved doing that, and I knew if I kept myself under the table and out of sight it was likely that the talk would get looser. More interesting. Someone might swear. Oh, the red lipstick marks they left on their coffee cups, the way they were used to their bosoms! I was waiting so hard to grow up. It was a job, waiting, when you were eleven. Every morning you looked at your face in the mirror to see if the babyness had gone away. Every night in the bathtub, you stretched your legs out before you, seeing if they were longer. They felt longer.

It was a Saturday morning, that time in my grandmother's kitchen. Sammy, the parakeet she kept on a TV tray by the kitchen window, was chirping happily. He liked the little symphony of voices he was hearing. He was very excited, you could tell, because he got a drink often out of his water dish – he always drank a lot of water when he was excited. His dish was one of those hooded glass ones, designs of lines on it. I thought it looked like a miniature urinal. I wondered how he could tell the difference. Later, he would die from flying into a pan where my grandmother was frying chicken. You couldn't help but smile from the irony, even though you felt terrible for poor Sammy.

My grandmother was getting ready to tell fortunes from tea leaves; she always did this before her daughters washed her hair. She was vain about her psychic abilities, but she was even more vain about her hair, and she had reason to be. It was long and thick and silvery white, and she had it washed weekly in her kitchen sink and then combed and combed and combed by her team of daughters. When it was dry, it would be twisted into the complicated arrangement she wore – part braid, part bun, part French twist. It would last a week, and then the daughters would all come to wash it again – and to see each other and gab, too, of course. My mother was always close to all her sisters, and she always felt badly that she wasn't able to produce one for me.

On that particular Saturday, my grandmother lifted the tablecloth and asked me if I would like my fortune read, too. I was honored, bumped my head hard on the way out from under the table, so eager was I to be included in this. I stood by her chair – it was the fifties kind of chair, I remember, red plastic Naugahyde with chrome trim and studs – and I had my fingers looped through the metal semicircle at the top of the chair and I was squeezing it because I was in love with Eric Underman and no one knew but me and I was scared my grandmother would say something about it and she did. She looked up at me and said, "Well! Your boyfriend likes you, too."

There was a loud and immediate response from my aunties – a chorus of "Oh!"s and "Ah-ha!"s and I was mortified, but I was also proud. At last, I was moving into the circle of mysterious, scented womanhood. Soon I could sit at the table with them. I could swear. I had it planned, already. "That SOB," I'd say.

But after my fortune was read, I went back under the table to dream about what I'd say to Eric the next time I saw him. I didn't pay attention anymore to the low chatter that went on in the kitchen. Those exchanges that used to be as delicious to me as the scent of warm bread became suddenly mundane. The next Saturday, I didn't go with my mother to wash her mother's hair. I stayed home, hoping to run into Eric, and I did. We were both on bikes. I offered him a butterscotch LifeSaver, and he took it; and I wrote about that supercharged exchange in my white leather diary and then hid it in a new place.

Now I see myself so ready to be back in that kitchen, to take my grandmother's heavy hair in my hands and whisper into her ear, "Why did you kick Grandpa out of the house?" She did kick him out for a while, for a period of a few months, when she was in her fifties. No one ever talked about why she did that, but I see myself asking her about it *now, and I see her answering me. "Well," she'd say. "I couldn't leave, so he had to. Until I was through it." Isn't that possible? I think it is. She didn't have the option of a trip away. So she created an artificial distance.*

I stopped at a lemonade stand today. I never can pass one by. There was a little girl working it, maybe ten, long blonde ponytail, blue glasses. She had a lawn chair to sit in when business was slow, but when she saw me pulling over, she stood up professionally. "May I help you?" she asked, when I was too far away to answer without shouting. I held up a finger. When I got to the stand, I said, "Yes, I'd like a lemonade. How much is it?"

"Fifty cents," she said.

I was disappointed. I thought it was too much. I thought it would have been cuter if it had been five or ten cents.

"Fifty cents, huh?" I said.

And she, unblinking, said, "Yes."

I paid for the lemonade and she poured me some, then watched me drink it. "Want another one?" she asked, when I was done. I said oh no, that was plenty, that was just right. "What if I had some cookies out here," she said. "Would you have bought one?"

I considered this. "What kind?"

"Chocolate chip AND peanut butter," she said, and I said well, of course. She pulled a fat tablet from behind the stand, wrote in it. I asked her if she were taking notes on how to improve business. No, she said, she'd just gotten an idea for a poem. Later, she'd write it. I said oh, you write

poetry? Wrote it and sold it too, she said. Sold it with the lemonade, but she was out of poems for today, she usually did run out of them before lemonade. I asked her how much the poems were. She said fifty cents. I said okay, I'll give you fifty cents if you'll do one for me right now. She smiled, then said, but I have to watch for customers and if one comes, I'll have to stop. Neither of us liked that idea. Tell you want, I said, I'll watch the stand. All right, she said, and she went to sit at the base of a nearby tree.

I sat in the lawn chair and I admit to feeling a certain nervousness. How much should I pour? What if I do it wrong? But this passed, and eventually I sat back in the chair and thought, maybe she should slice a lemon, have it floating on top. Maybe she should branch out a little, have iced tea, too. I snuck a look at her now and then. She was concentrating fiercely, her face drawn inward as though she were in pain. She scratched at her ankle, then stuck her finger inside her sneaker near the arch of her foot and kept it there, as though now she were plugged into herself. After a while she called over, "What's your name?" And I told her Nan and a light came into her face. "Good," she said, "that's good," and she started writing. In a few minutes she came over and handed me a poem. It was about crossing a bridge over a river full of monsters, into a land of purple fields and yellow clouds. I loved most of all the last line, where she said my name was Empress Nana Exsanna Popana. Best fifty cents I ever spent. I told her so, too. "Oh," she said, tightening her ponytail, prettily embarrassed. "Yeah."

Dear Martin,

Last night I dreamed I was here, dreaming. It was very odd, waking up and trying to separate things. I felt hungry and I sat on the side of the bed thinking, where should I go? A diner, for two over easy? A bakery, for a blueberry muffin? The motel had a small restaurant attached, for breakfast only, "The Good Morning Café," it was called. I wasn't sure if that would be a good idea. Some things wonderfully named have terrible-tasting food.

But I did go, and I sat at the counter and after I ordered my Western omelet I read a local newspaper. There was a photograph on the front page of a group of people sitting around a picnic table, all of them older. It was the sixtieth reunion of the local high school, McKinley High. I thought probably this small crowd was there to see who was still alive. But when I looked closer at the faces, I didn't see any mournful satisfaction. I saw that they were looking at each other in a way that bypassed all those years. The football player was still seeing the pink-cheeked girl in the pleated skirt, and vice versa.

I remember a man whose wife died a gruesome death telling me that he was amazed by people who were amazed that he could take care of her at the end, that he could keep her at home and offer ice chips to cracked lips that no longer said anything comprehensible, that he could uncomplainingly change sheets a few times a day because they had been soiled for this awful reason or that. "But I saw her the way she used to be," he told me. "I mean, through the way that she was now. Through it and including it, actually, it was all always her." And I remember thinking, that was a lucky woman. Never mind that she died a horrible death – we all are faced with that possibility. What mattered was that at the end, someone who loved her sat by her, saying, I see you.

I noticed this morning that the veins on my hands don't look the way they used to. And the first thought that came to me was, should I do something about this? What do they do about this, vein stripping, is that what it is? This came to me automatically, even after what I believe I've started to learn. But it's so silly. So tiresome, that kind of thinking, and so self-defeating. If I get a face lift, the skin on my back will still sag, and soften. If I get my eyes done, my joints will still ache. Life has its way, and it seems to me now that the object might only be to learn how to be graceful, to understand the value of a deep kind of acceptance.

There are those who have catastrophic events happen in their lives when they are young. Early on, they lose so much. But for the rest of us, those of us who have the luxury of being called normal, there is only the slow loss of what we see as our prime. First the half-glasses, then the hair growing where it shouldn't, then the memory that walks half a step away from you, the way you cannot quite find the word, it goes racing by you like a fast bird in flight. "Don't get old," my father's mother told me, old herself. She meant that I should spare myself this most personal of griefs. But why not get old, when what it means is more time with all that is here? Why not relish retirement when it means an alarm clock does not wake you anymore? You can take in the morning light as an offering, lie still for a while with a square patch of sun lying across your chest. The day is blank and up to you. You can twist yourself in your sheets for the pleasure of the pull, knowing it will not make you late for anything. You can dress in jeans and roll down a hill, terrified all over again, though for different reasons having to do with old bones. You leave the high place, tumble toward the bottom. Beneath you, the grass flattens, acknowledging your presence, then rises again, as though you were never there. You see this, now; and it seems to me that if you want to, you can understand the rightness of it. What I mean is, when you learn to turn from the mirror, when you look up from your hands, you have a chance to see a garden truly, because you are not in your own way. I say this because I read a poem by a farmer to his wife where he talked about that, Martin, and it made me realize I would love to circle a garden with you, both of us seeing the same thing at the same time. I remember when we first met and you gave me a bite of your sandwich and you said, "I hope you taste it the same as me." I thought it was thrilling that you said that. (I thought it was sexual, too.) I know that feeling. I have wanted you to see out of my eyes so many times. More than ever, lately.

I have been waiting to be without anxiety before I start home. But I think I am waiting for something that will never come. I mean that all relationships are fraught with anxiety, even those we have with ourselves. We live on a planet that never stops turning and we are witness to the theater of the seasons. How can we expect a relationship to not change? Any change makes us anxious, it just does – given the opportunity, we will nearly all of us sit in the same chair, every time. It is a tender thing, the way we always seek reassurance, the way we are never too old to reach for the outstretched hand.

I know there's a chance you'll be angry at me, Martin. Outraged, even, and wanting to sit in your den and sulk as soon as you see me. But there's also a chance you'll be glad I left, and glad I returned. There's a chance you'll come to the driveway to meet me before I've gotten fully out of the car, and offer to carry in my heaviest bag. I confess I hope for that. I have imagined it, as I have imagined you sitting at the kitchen table drinking your coffee and putting down the newspaper, to remember me.

However it is that you feel, know that I am coming home to you now. I'm not stopping for anything but sleep, bathrooms, and meals. When I left, I couldn't wait to get away. Now I can't wait to get back.

So here I come, Martin, changed a bit it's true. I am Nana Exsanna Popana, woman and child. I am every age I ever was and I always will be and I know that now. I am coming home and I want nothing more than to try to tell you everything. I'm so eager to see you, Martin. Perhaps we'll see each other.

Love,
Nan

Also by Elizabeth Berg and available from Arrow Books

TRUE TO FORM

In this warm and engaging novel, *New York Times* best-selling author Elizabeth Berg revisits the heroine she so lovingly brought to life in *Durable Goods* and *Joy School*.

It is 1961, and thirteen-year-old Katie is facing a summer full of conflict. First, instead of letting her find her own work for the season, Katie's father has arranged for two less than ideal baby-sitting jobs. Worse, Katie has been forcibly inducted into the "loser" Girl Scout troop organized by her only friend Cynthia's controlling and clueless mother. A much anticipated visit to her former home in Texas and ex-best friend Cherylanne proves disappointing. And then comes an act of betrayal that leaves Katie questioning her views on friendship, on her ability not to take those she loves for granted, and most important, on herself.

"Savvy, wry, and sharply observant . . . Berg's graceful and deceptively simple prose is laced with clear-eyed insights . . . deft and inspiring." *The Denver Post*

"Berg knows her characters intimately . . . she gets under their skin and leaves the reader with an indelible impression of lives challenged and changed." *The Seattle Times*

"With great tenderness and exquisite vision, Elizabeth Berg details the small truths and grand mysteries of the human heart." Nora Roberts

Arrow Books
0 09 944688 X
£6.99

Read on for chapter one of
True to Form

It is the first Sunday evening of the summer, the sky an ash rose color and losing its light to night. I am sitting on the floor in my room with a mirror propped up against a stack of magazines, setting my hair according to the directions in *Modern Style*. If I do it right, I will get a perfect flip. I just need to sleep in such a way that the rollers do not become pushed out of place, as they usually do. Either they get pushed out of place or I take them all out in the middle of the night. I don't know why. I don't even remember doing it, I just wake up and there the rollers are, thrown down on the floor. I guess my sleep self and my awake self don't agree about beauty.

The radio is turned on low to "Moody River," and my question is, Why did she kill herself if the guy was just a friend? And also, how can Pat Boone be singing so smoothly if his heart is broken? He sounds like Perry Como singing "Magic Moments" when he should be sounding like Brenda Lee sobbing, "I'm sorry, sooo sorry."

I am thinking about how tomorrow I will lie out on

a towel in the yard, slicked up with baby oil to get going on my tan. I like it when you lie there for a long time and feel the sun's heat like a red thing behind your lids. You see a map of your own veins, and then when you open your eyes the view is bleached a bit of its colors. When I was nine years old someone told me you must never look at the sun straight on because it could make you blind. This made me go right outside and stare up at it, and when my eyes protested and shut automatically, I held my lids open until my eyes burned and watered so much I had to stop. I did not go blind. I do have to wear glasses, but I was wearing them before I stared at the sun. I am this way, sometimes, that I just have to find things out for myself.

I have a feeling percolating under my skin that says this will be a really important summer. Just a feeling that doesn't go away. I think sometimes I am a little psychic, like my grandmother who could read tea leaves. She would sit at the kitchen table with her beautiful white hair up in a bun, and she would be wearing an apron that sagged over her bosom like another bosom. She would stare into the cup for a long time, and nobody talked; even the air seemed to hold still. Then she would look up, and her blue eyes would seem clearer and not quite her own. She would settle her shoulders, and, in a low and intimate voice, tell people things about their lives. I thought for a long time she was a gypsy queen, but my mind just made that up;

she was really just a woman from England who married my grandfather from Ireland. She was a housewife who made good gravy and kept a parakeet in her kitchen.

Once, when I was in third grade, my grandmother read tea leaves for me. My mother was there, and her sisters, my aunts Rose and Betty, were there, too. I remember I was so nervous I sat under the kitchen table, and my grandmother had to tell me things without looking at me. She said I had a boyfriend, which was true, Billy Harris was his name, and I got all embarrassed even though no one could see me. Then she told me he liked me too, which was not so true, since if you asked him, "Do you like Katie Nash?" he would have said, "Who?"

I miss my aunts a lot. Since my mother died a couple of years ago, I never see them anymore. We used to go and visit for a week or so every summer. Rose was very prim and proper, but full of a warm love. When I used to stay there, my cousins and I washed up for bed at night in a dishpan at the kitchen sink, and Aunt Rose made sure we got our ears good. Ivory soap, she used, those floating cakes bigger than a kid's whole hand. She made plain dinners but they were the kind of food a person always enjoys. Like just meat loaf from the recipe on the back of the oatmeal box, served with mashed potatoes, butter filling the little well in the middle, and some green beans from the can, all served on an embroidered tablecloth. Her sheets smelled like outside, and everybody used to say you could eat from her kitchen floor. I used to think, *Why would you want to do that?* and I would imagine my uncle Harry sitting there cross-legged with his napkin tucked into his shirt, leaning over awkwardly to lift his scrambled eggs from the linoleum.

Aunt Betty was a wild woman, that's what she called herself. She told me she was engaged to another man when my uncle Jim proposed to her. She wore a lot of makeup and smoked constantly and painted her fingernails and toenails blood red. She and my uncle were very social, and I never saw anyone look as glamorous as she did when they went out. She would wake up her children for a meteor shower or a good sunrise, and she was always asking them to tell her things they learned in school; she thought her children were wonderful. Every Sunday morning, she would make Monkey Bread, and there was always enough for everyone.

My dad doesn't want to visit my aunts anymore. I guess he has a new life now with my stepmother, Ginger, and the aunts just don't figure in. Sometimes I get mail from them: a joke card from Betty; a card with Jesus on it from Rose. They both call me Honey, which makes for an inside curl of pleasure. I thought I would always go and see them, every summer.

Well, you never know what life will turn out to be. Sometimes when I lie in bed at night, I think of bad things that can happen and how much we can never know, and it's so scary. It's like taking the lid off a box that's in front of you all the time, but usually you leave it alone. But every now and then, you take the lid off and you look in and the box is so dark and deep and full of writhing possibilities it gives you the shivers.

I lean back against my bed, let out a big breath, and look around my bedroom. I am used to it now, which probably means it's about time to move. Every time I get used to something, it's time to leave it. "We have orders," my father will say, and that's that, we're on the way to wherever the army tells us to go.

I like this room. It feels more private than any place I've ever had, situated the way it is at the end of the hall. If my sister, Diane, were still living with us, she would have gotten this room; she always got the best room. But she lives by herself in California now, because she ran away when she was eighteen. We talk about twice a month, and once in a while she comes to visit, but mostly it is just no good between her and my father; it never was. My father was always fierce, but after my mother died it seemed like he got a lot worse. And Diane finally just left. He never talks about it, but I know he is sorry. One thing my stepmother has done is to make my father a little softer, not so mean. It's odd; I think he loved my mother more, but he treats Ginger better. And I think I know why. It is because she is not as nice to him as my mother was. She pushes back, sometimes.

She draws a line and says don't you cross this. Now you tell me why someone is nicer to the person who treats him worse.

My favorite place in my room is my desk drawer. In it is a little figure of a bird all covered with jewels. I don't think they're real jewels, but maybe they are. It was given to me by a boy I did not know, for no reason. It was a while ago, just after my mother had died, and I was sitting out by myself in the middle of a field on a summer day, and the boy appeared out of nowhere. He was younger than I, I thought – smaller, at least, and so I wasn't afraid. I said, "Hey," and he said nothing back. "What are you doing?" I asked, and again he said nothing. I asked him if he spoke English, and he just smiled and shrugged. I stared at him for a while, and then I patted the ground. He sat next to me, his knees drawn up under his chin, and together we watched the movement of the breeze through the tall weeds, the lazy shifting of the gigantic cumulus clouds that filled the sky that day, and, once, the magical hovering of a dragonfly, colored metallic blue. We only pointed at things, but it was a good conversation. We sat for a good fifteen or twenty minutes, and then the boy got up to leave. But first he took the bird out of his pocket and gave it to me. I was amazed by his generosity, but I am ashamed to say that I made no move at all to refuse that gift. It is the main thing in my drawer, because it was a miracle and it came without asking. Sometimes when I think of that boy, I think, Wait, was he mute? And sometimes I think – the thought very small and private – Was he an angel? And sometimes I think, in a way that makes me feel like bawling, Was he my mother? That thought is the smallest and most private of all, and it lives in my heart, and it will never be told to anyone.

Also in my drawer is a photo of baby pigs. I remember them vaguely from a time we lived on a farm in Indiana. I think I was three. I remember being barefoot, standing on the wooden rail of a fence, looking down at those pigs. I wanted them to be my dollies; I wanted to wheel them in a carriage, put bonnets on their heads, feed them from bottles, and cover them when they slept. But they were not babies, they were pigs. So I only watched them lie by their mother in their neat, pink row; and I watched them take their grunty little steps around the sty.

I have some rocks I cracked open and kept for their gorgeous insides. I have some acorns, because look what comes from them. I have a pressed flower, a rose I would still call pink, even though its edges have turned tea-colored. I have pictures of beautiful things cut out of magazines: a willow tree next to a river, a kitchen lit up by morning sun, a monarch on a red poppy, a herd of sheep on a hill in Ireland, a wooden, straight-back chair positioned by a window with a blowing white curtain. I have a lot of pictures of dogs, too. I would like to have seven dogs.

I have something that I drew, a woman's face that is full of sorrow. And it looks like a real picture that an artist did. It looks that way to me. And the thing is, I don't know how to draw. I was sitting at my desk one day, my head in my hands, and I had that middle ache that is just the pain that comes with being alive sometimes, that kind of personal despair. I don't know why it comes, but I know it used to get my mother too. Every once in a while, she would sit so still, her hands in her lap, and she would have a little smile on her face that was not really a smile. What's wrong? I once asked, and she looked up quickly and she saw that I saw. After that, she would usually close herself in her bedroom until it was over – it never took that long, really. She didn't like for anyone to see her that way. She didn't want anyone to know.

But I had that same kind of feeling one day, that veil of sadness between me and the world, and I had a piece of paper in front of me and I drew that woman's face like I was in a dream, like someone else was borrowing my hand. And I have never shown it to anyone, and I have never drawn anything good since then, either.

Lately, I have begun writing a lot more poems, and I have been saving them in my drawer. And it's funny, the same thing happens, about someone else borrowing my hand. I get a feeling; I step off into space; and a thing makes up itself.

I have red lipstick in my drawer that was my

mother's, with the mark of her mouth on it. I have a rhinestone button I found outside, feathers from birds, pennies that mean good luck. I have a box of crayons that I intend never to use, I just like to look at them all perfect and read the names of the colors out loud, and I like to smell them deep, like I smell the test papers at school that have just come off the mimeograph machine. I have some torn-out hairdos that I would like to get, if my hair will ever grow really long instead of acting paralyzed.

Sometimes I think, What if I died and someone looked in my drawer? I wonder what they would understand about me. Probably not so much – for one thing, they would get the crayons wrong. I think, actually, that none of us understands anyone else very well, because we're all too shy to show what matters the most. If you ask me, it's a major design flaw. We ought to be able to say, Here, look what I am. I think it would be quite a relief.

Read on for the opening chapters of
Until the Real Thing
Comes Along

PROLOGUE

This is how you play the house game:

Go for a drive to somewhere you've never been. At the point when the spirit moves you, start looking for your house. You can choose whatever you want, at any time; and once you choose it, it is yours. One caveat: after you've made a selection, you can't change your mind. If you pick the white colonial with the pristine picket fence and then in the next block you see an even better colonial, it's too late; you must stay with your first choice.

I started playing this game as a little girl, and I still play it. And I always pick too early, so it almost always happens that a much grander choice comes along. I might be expected to feel regret at such a moment, but I never do. I can admit to the superiority of another house; I can admire it and see every way in which it is better than my first choice, but I am never sorry. I know a lot of people have a hard time believing this, but it's true. I know a lot of people think it's an odd characteristic, too, but I have to say it is something I like about myself. It is, in fact, what I like most.

I used to think that the best thing to do when you had the blues was to soak in a bathtub full of hot water, submerge yourself so that only the top half of your head was in the outer world. You could feel altered and protected. Weightless. You could feel mysterious, like a crocodile, who is bound up with the wisdom of the natural world and does not concern herself with the number of dates she has per month or the biological time clock. You could feel purified by the rising steam. Best of all, you could press a washrag across your chest, and it would feel like the hand of your mother when you were little and suffering from a cold, and she'd lay her flat palm on you to draw the sickness out.

The problem with the bathtub method is that you have to keep fooling with the faucet to keep the water temperature right, and that breaks the healing spell. Besides that, as soon as you get out of the tub the solace disappears as quickly as the water, and you are left with only your annoying lobster self, staring blankly into the mirror.

These days I believe that museums are the place to

go to lose your sorrow. Fine-art museums with high ceilings and severe little boxes mounted on the wall to measure the level of humidity; rooms of furniture displayed so truly the people seem to have just stepped out for a minute; glass cases full of ancient pottery in the muted colors of old earth. There are mummies, wearing the ultimate in long-lasting eyeliner; old canvases that were held between the hands of Vermeer; new canvases with emphatic smears of paint. The cafés have pastry as artful as anything else in the building; gift shops are stocked with jewelry modeled after the kind worn by Renaissance women – the garnet-and-drop-pearl variety. I buy that kind of jewelry, in love with its romantic history and the sight of it against the black velvet. Then I bring it home and never wear it because it looks stupid with everything I have. But it is good to own anyway, for the pleasure of laying it on the bedspread and then sitting beside it, touching it.

What I like most about museums is that the efforts of so many people remain so long after they are gone. They made their marks. If you are an artist, you can hope to achieve that. If you are not an artist, you believe that having children is the closest you'll come.

Well, that's what I believe. And anyway, I have always preferred the company of children; I just like to be around them. Whenever my large family gets together on holidays, I sit at the kids' card table. It's so much more relaxing, what with the way the dishes are plastic, and manners of any kind optional. So much more interesting, too – no talk about current events, no holding forth by any overweight, overeducated aunt or uncle. There is talk only about things that are astonishing. Facts about the red ant, say, or the elaborate retelling of an unfortunate incident, such as the one where a kid vomited on the teacher's desk.

I always thought I'd have five or six children, and I have imagined so many lovely domestic scenes featuring me and my offspring. Here we are outside on a hot summer day, running through the sprinkler. The children wear bright fluorescent bathing suits in pink and green and yellow; I wear cutoffs and a T-shirt. There is fruit salad in the refrigerator. Later, I will let the older kids squirt whipped cream for the younger ones; then, if they pester me enough in the right way, I'll let them squirt it into their mouths – and mine.

Or here I am at the grocery store, my married hands unloading graham crackers and packages of American cheese that have already been broken into due to the eager appetite of the toddler in the carriage, who is dressed in tiny OshKosh overalls over a striped shirt. His fine hair, infused with gold and red, curls up slightly at the back of his neck. His swinging feet are chubby and bare; he has flung his sneakers and socks on top of the family-size pack of chicken breasts. His brothers and sisters are in school. Later in the afternoon, he will stand at the living-room window, watching for them to come home, squealing and bending his knees in a little joy dance when he sees them marching down the sidewalk toward him, swinging their lunch boxes in high, bright-colored arcs.

I have imagined myself making dinner while my dark-haired daughter sits at the kitchen table. She is making me a picture of a house with window boxes, choosing crayons with slow care. She is wearing yellow turtle barrettes in her hair, and a bracelet she made from string. "Hey, Mommy," she says, "do you want flowers on the ground, too?" Oh yes, I say. Sure. "Me too," she says. We smile.

I have imagined a fleshy constellation of small children and me, spread out and napping on my big bed while the newest baby sleeps in her crib. The pulled-down shades lift with the occasional breeze, then slap gently back against the windowsill. If you listen carefully, you can hear the small breathing sounds of the children, their soothing, syncopated rhythms. There is no other sound, not even from the birds; the afternoon is holding its finger to its lips. All the children have blankets and all of them are sucking their thumbs. All of them are read to every night after their baths. All of them think they are the favorite. None of them has ever had an illness of any kind, or ever will. (I mean, as long as I'm imagining.)

What I never imagined was the truth: me at thirty-six years of age, lying around on top of my made bed on a beautiful winter afternoon with shades pulled for an entirely different reason, thinking, Why didn't I marry Johnny Tranchilla? So he was shorter than I was. He was very handsome and very romantic. He had black curly hair and naturally red lips. He sent me a love note in the mail after our first date and he was only nineteen, how brave! His father was loaded. He wore Weejuns with no socks. I could have been happy. Then I go on through the rest of my short list, thinking of the men I might possibly have married. Ron Anderson, who became a mildly famous artist and now lives in a huge A-frame in the Rocky Mountains with his blond wife, who is more beautiful than I'll ever be but not as much fun, I can guarantee it. She would never have broken into the planetarium like I did with Ron, would never have entered into the famous mustard-and-catsup fight at D.J.'s diner at three in the morning.

There was Tim Connor too, who was quiet and tender and reliable – not exciting, but one grows tired of that after one is, oh, say, ninety-five. Frank Olds became a neurosurgeon! I could have lived in material comfort instead of making dinners out of soda crackers and cottage cheese and repeatedly showing houses to people who will never buy any of them.

The reason I didn't marry any of the various men I might have is always the same: Ethan Allen Gaines. I fell in love with him in sixth grade, and I never, never stopped loving him, not even after we tried to have a serious relationship in our late twenties and failed, and he took me out to dinner to a very nice place to break off our engagement and told me it was because he was gay. "Oh, Ethan," I said, "that's okay, I'll marry you anyway." It was as inadvertent and embarrassing as a piece of meat flying out of my mouth. Ethan nodded, looked away. And then back at me. And I knew that was the end of that. Knew it in my head, anyway. The heart is always a different matter. I kept the ring. It lives in a box as beautiful as it is.

"I told you," my friend Elaine said the day after we broke up. "I *told* you! Who else would keep rolled-up towels on their bathroom sink?"

"They were *hand* towels," I said.

". . . And?"

"A lot of people roll up their hand towels."

"Patty. It wasn't just the towels."

"*I* know," I said. "I know!"

But I hadn't known. I hadn't let myself.

Because consider this: once Ethan and I were at a lake and he rented a boat because I said I had never learned how to row. He told me what to do, made me get in alone, and watched from shore, shouting encouragement. I got stuck. I dropped an oar. Ethan was telling me how to come in with one oar, but I was just going around in circles. "I can't do it!" I yelled. He put a hand to his forehead, shielding his eyes, and yelled back, "Yes, you can!" But I couldn't. And so he waded out to me in his beautiful new brown tweed pants and white sweater and pulled me in. And I sat, hanging onto both sides of the boat, watching the sun in his yellow hair and the moving muscles of his back. And when he got me in, we sat in the grass and he was wringing out his pants and sweater and dumping water from his shoes and I said I was so sorry, I knew how expensive those clothes were – they were from Anthony's, a very exclusive men's shop that served you Chivas in a cut-crystal glass while you fingered linens and silks. Ethan asked if I wanted to go shopping and I said sure, I'll buy you some new clothes, but not from Anthony's. He said no, I'll buy an outfit for both of us. I said, I ruined your pants! Why would you buy me an outfit? And he said because you can't row a boat.

The day before that, we'd been to see a movie with an exquisitely sad ending, the kind that makes your insides feel made of glass. My throat ached when the lights came up; I wanted to just run out of there so I wouldn't have to hear anything anyone said. Ethan's face seemed full of what I felt, too. "Run," he whispered, and we did. We ran to his car and slammed the doors and sat still, staring straight ahead and saying not one word. Then I looked over at him and he took my hand and said, "I know."

On the night Ethan told me he was gay, I said that admitting it must be a very liberating experience, that it must feel good. He said it did in many ways, but it hurt him that he had to hurt me. I said, well, we would always be best friends, wouldn't we? He said of course.

I didn't cry until I came home and climbed into the bathtub. Then I sobbed for a good twenty minutes. And then I leaned back, laid the washrag over my chest, inhaled the steamy air, and thought about when Ethan had come over when I was sick, just a few weeks earlier. He'd made chicken soup and three kinds of Jell-O, brought with him a variety of cheeses and crackers and fruit. He'd treated me with a tenderness that was somehow too competent. I'd watched him, longing for him to come over to me, kneel down, knock over my ginger ale, ignore it, take my hand, and say, "If you ever die, I'll kill myself." But he didn't do that. He ran his hand sweetly over my forehead, went to adjust the flame under the soup; then, frowning, flipped through the channels on the television. He covered me with a quilt he'd laundered, patted my feet affectionately, then made a phone call. I felt as though he were zipped into a self that was hiding the real him – I could get close, but not *there*. I had put it down to a normal kind of male reticence, the kind that has a woman sigh and put her hand on her hip and call a girlfriend. I had believed that with the trust and intimacy of marriage it would get better – he would open himself completely to me.

But that night, with my engagement ring newly off my finger (though the stubborn indentation of it remained), I slid deeper into the water and thought about all the times Ethan and I had made love. Then I thought about those times again, and saw them true. I pulled the washrag up over my face. Beneath it, I think I was blushing.

Also by Elizabeth Berg and available from Arrow Books

TALK BEFORE SLEEP

"Elizabeth Berg [is] a gifted storyteller with a fine sense of pace and phrasing, as well as a splendid ear for dialogue" *Boston Sunday Globe*

"Until that moment, I hadn't realized how much I'd been needing to meet someone I might be able to say everything to."

They met at a party. It was hate at first sight. Ruth was far too beautiful, too flamboyant. Not at all Ann's kind of person. Until a chance encounter in the bathroom led to an alliance of souls. Soon they were sharing hankies during the late showing of *Sophie's Choice*, wolfing down sundaes sodden with whipped cream, telling truths of marriage, mortality, and love, secure in a kind of intimacy no man could ever know. Only best friends understand devil's food cake for breakfast when nothing else will do. After years of shared secrets, guilty pleasures, family life and divorce, they face a crisis that redefines the meaning of friendship and unconditional love.

"A searing story of friendship and death . . . A triumph of creativity." *Time Out*

"A rich coming-of-age novel . . . A luminous work." *New York Times Books Review*

"Tender and irreverent by turns, it offers mature, intelligent and buoyant spirit, like a very good friend." *Houston Post*

"Entertaining, finely crafted . . . Elizabeth Berg tackles serious issues with grace." *San Francisco Chronicle*

Arrow Books
0 09 945172 7
£6.99

RANGE OF MOTION

"The love story of the year" *Detroit Free Press*

"I can tell you how it happened. It's easy to say how it happened. He walked past a building and a huge chunk of ice fell off the roof, and it hit him in the head. This is Chaplinesque, right? People start to laugh when I tell them . . ."

As Jay Berman lingers in a coma, his young wife, Lainey, is the only one who believes he will recover. While he lays motionless, she hopes to reach him by offering reminders of the ordinary life they shared – sweet-smelling flowers, his softly textured shirt, spices from their kitchen. And throughout her ordeal, Lainey is sustained by her relationships with two very special women, each of whom teaches her about the enduring bond of friendship and the genuine power of hope.

"Elegant . . . limitless in its philosophical scope."
Los Angeles Times

"This is the terrifically talented Berg at her best." *People*

"A luminous, bittersweet, almost mystical meditation on the unexpected, often hidden, joys found in the least likely of places." *San Francisco Chronicle Book Review*.

Arrow Books
0 09 945173 5
£6.99

OPEN HOUSE

"Maybe Freud didn't know the answer to what women want, but Elizabeth Berg does." *USA Today*

"You are bending over the dryer, pulling out the still-warm sheets, and the knowledge walks up your backbone. You stare at the man you love and you are staring at nothing; he is gone before he is gone."

When Samantha Morrow's husband leaves her and her eleven-year-old son she is faced with the terrifying prospect of having to recreate her whole life. After a few faltering steps she starts to put the pieces into place. She opens her house to a series of lodgers who each in their eccentric way help her to see herself. She fends off her mother, whose idea of getting over a failed marriage is to get a pedicure and get out there dating.

And she makes a friend, King, an MIT graduate turned handyman, who shows her that she has the ability to make her own future and her own happiness . . .

"Berg has an ability to capture the way women think, feel and speak . . . With her quirky characters and precise observations, Berg sits somewhere between Anne Tyler and Alice Hoffman . . . The details and emotions in *Open House* are sometimes heartwrenching, sometimes hilarious." *Chicago Sun-Times*

"Smart, witty and so emotionally taut and true that I couldn't put it down . . . Berg shows a sparkling ability to distil complex human emotions into a few hundred pages of clear, evocative prose." *Journal Sentinel*

Arrow Books
0 09 946126 9
£6.99

NEVER CHANGE

"Heartwrenching . . . hilarious . . . Berg sits
somewhere between Anne Tyler and Alice Hoffman"
Chicago Sun-Times

*"You know people like me. I'm the one who sat in the hall
selling tickets to the prom but never going, the one
everybody liked but no one wanted to be with."*

Myra Lipinsky has endured the isolation of her middle life
by immersing herself in her career as a visiting nurse. She
considers herself reasonably content until Chip Reardon,
the too-good-to-be-true golden boy she adored from afar
whilst at high school, is assigned to be her new patient.
Now, as they find themselves engaged in a poignant
redefinitions of roles, Myra discovers that true love can
blossom even in the most difficult of circumstances.

"Never Change is sad, yes, but it's funny, too – a Berg
trademark . . . She shows that life is most beautiful in the
moments that come and pass away again, a lesson often
learned long after high school."
Atlanta Journal-Constitution

"There's something compelling about the way Berg
knows her characters intimately, how she gets under
their skin and leaves the reader with an indelible
impression of lives challenged and changed."
Seattle Times

"With great tenderness and exquisite vision, Elizabeth
Berg details the small truths and grand mysteries of the
human heart." Nora Roberts

Arrow Books
0 09 946127 7
£6.99

JOY SCHOOL

"Hilarious and heartbreaking."
San Francisco Examiner & Chronicle

Katie has relocated to Missouri with her distant, occasionally abusive father, and she feels very much alone: her
much-loved mother is dead; her new school is unaccepting
of her; and her only friends fall far short of being ideal
companions. When she accidentally falls through the ice
while skating, she meets Jimmy. He is handsome, far older
than she, and married, but she is entranced. As their
relationship unfolds, so too does Katie's awareness of the
pain and intensity first love can bring.

"A story that tugs at the heartstrings . . . With humour
and an eye for telling detail, Berg conveys the way each
unpromising element of Katie's life ultimately offers her
more than she had anticipated." *People*

"A funny, sweet, coming-of-age narrative . . . Its heart
will remind Berg's fans why her writing is so eminently
likeable." *Chicago Tribune*

"Berg's style works beautifully – deceptively simple,
conversational, and hip." *USA Today*

Arrow Books
0 09 945175 1
£6.99